PANIC AT THE PIER

A WHODUNIT PET COZY MYSTERY SERIES BOOK 1

MEL MCCOY

To Linda —

[signature]

CHAPTER 1

Sarah Shores was startled when she felt a tongue hit her cheek. She gripped the steering wheel of her Corolla, focusing to keep it from veering toward the sandy shoulder. Driving for nearly four hours since her last pitstop, on her way from New York City to Florida, the slobber had shocked her into alertness.

Taking her eyes off the road for a moment, she caught the yellow lab's head popping between her and the passenger seat. His eighty pounds of muscle and fur were hard to miss.

"Take it easy, Rugby. We're almost there."

She took the exit off the highway and saw the billboard.

"Cascade Cove," she said, smiling. "Glad to be back."

It was true; she needed this vacation from the city, from her stressful job teaching. The politics were definitely getting to her, holding her back from the teaching and nurturing she really wanted to provide to her young students. Instead, she often felt more like a caseworker fighting against the system. A couple of bad-apple superiors made the job more difficult than it needed to be.

She shook her head, ridding her mind of those thoughts. Today was the start of her vacation and there was no use in dwelling on the stress back in the city.

Getting closer to Cascade Cove, she felt her tension melt away. It was ironic—she'd spent her formative years wishing to be anywhere else but in that sleepy, beachside town, when she'd visited her grandparents each summer. She had dreamed of the hustle and bustle of a place that never slept. Now, deprived of sleep, she couldn't wait to downshift into a more relaxing life, even if only for two weeks.

Along a narrow two-lane road, Sarah made her way into town, feeling her long brown hair waving in the late-spring breeze. She inhaled, taking in the salt-water aroma that she'd missed so much.

After a quarter-mile or so, she saw the abundance of vacation homes flanking the road—all looked currently vacant, but soon, Sarah knew the area would be a bustle of activity.

Past the vacation homes, Sarah saw the beachgrass-topped dunes off to her left. Between them, she spotted the ocean, the waves lapping against the sand. Then she saw the start of the boardwalk that ran along the coast and parallel to the small beachside town. From the boardwalk, vacationers could easily access the many businesses that lined the main road of Cascade Cove. The main road itself was a top destination, as it featured many small shops, restaurants, and attractions.

"We're almost there," Sarah said to Rugby, who was panting in the back seat.

Overhead, a few seagulls squawked, the sound of their chatter mixing with the crashing of waves on the pristine beach. The sun warmed her skin as she approached the middle of the town, finally reaching her grandfather's business, Larry's Pawfect Boutique.

"Looks exactly the same," she said to Rugby, whose nose was pressed against the rear passenger window, fogging it up with each huff he made. In honesty, there were some differences from the last time she visited— the store's sign showed evidence of the years past; the latex paw-prints on the glass front door were crinkled on the edges, victims of the blistering summer sun. Sarah figured this coming summer would be their last before they needed to be replaced, but then she realized she'd thought that last summer.

Heaving a sigh of nostalgia, Sarah turned back to Rugby. "You haven't seen the crew in a while. Let's go, boy."

She got out of the car and opened the door for Rugby, who lumbered out and shook himself off. He tugged on the leash and led her along the sidewalk toward the entrance to the boutique.

Bells jingled above her head as she entered. Rugby darted toward the checkout counter, where her grandfather, Larry, stood smiling. He was a bespectacled man with gray, curly hair. A Persian cat rushed off the counter and dodged Rugby, a moment before collision. Rugby stopped abruptly, then sauntered toward the hesitant cat, lapping it lightly along the side of its head. The cat batted Rugby's nose, then darted away.

"Score one for Misty," Sarah said.

Larry smiled. "She misses this big lug, almost as much as I missed you."

"Aw, Grandpa. I missed you too."

Larry turned toward the back of the store, where the door to his office was slightly open, and yelled out, "Emma, your cousin's here."

Larry stepped out from behind the counter and hugged her. Sarah caught a whiff of his cologne, and she coughed lightly. Ending the embrace, she shook her head. "Still wearing that potent stuff?"

"Of course," Larry said, grasping the collar of his Hawaiian shirt and taking in the smell. He let out a long exhale. "I love it."

Sarah shook her head and smiled. "Grandma always used to complain about the smell. I take it she's coming around to it?"

"Not exactly. I'm only wearing it in full force since she's off working the cruise line."

"Again?"

"Can't keep that woman from what she loves. She tried to get me to come along this summer, but I can't stay away from this place. Plus, Emma would be all alone." Turning back toward the office, Larry called out again, louder this time. "Emma, did you hear me? Come on out—your cousin's here."

Not more than two seconds later, Emma came bolting out of the back office. Her eyes lit up like a Christmas tree, and she was all smiles. Her blonde hair was tied up in a ponytail that bobbed around as she bounded toward Sarah.

"Sarah!" Emma wrapped her arms around Sarah, almost knocking her off her feet. After a moment, she stepped back to eye up her cousin. "How are you? How was the drive here?"

Sarah smiled back. Growing up, they were insepara-ble, but lately, they had grown apart. While Sarah was building her career in the inner-city public school system, Emma had stayed behind with their grandfather. He'd taken her under his wing, showing her the ropes of how to run the boutique. Perhaps she was happy to escape the cold winters and decided to stick around. Sarah could understand the appeal.

"Long, as usual," Sarah said, giving her cousin another hug. "It's been forever since I've seen you, Em."

"Almost a year. You staying longer than two weeks this time?"

Before Sarah could answer, Rugby rushed by between them, Misty hot on his tail. The yellow lab's tongue flopped around as he raced away from his pursuer.

"I know what Rugby needs," Larry said, reaching into a plastic container that sat on the glass display case, with an open top that looked much like a small fish tank. He noodled around with his fingers—the sound of biscuits mingling with one another was effective at drawing Rugby back to them.

Larry pulled a biscuit from the container and held it down in Rugby's path. "Here, boy. Want a treat?"

Rugby's ears perked up at the T word, and he snatched the treat in one fell swoop, rushing away to enjoy it in privacy behind one of the display gondolas of handmade collars and leashes.

Larry looked back at Sarah. "These are the new biscuits I wanted to tell you about."

"Grandpa," Emma said before Sarah could reply, "don't forget we need to place another order with Fudderman's Bakery."

Sarah smirked. "Henry Fudderman is making dog treats now?"

Larry stepped toward a display of boxes and pulled one from a fully-stocked shelf. "That old coot's not just catering to people anymore. He's testing out these new treats with us, giving us exclusive rights to sell them in the Cove. Check these out: 'Fudderdog Treats.' Completely organic ingredients and homemade. They come in carrot, sweet potato, or peanut butter flavors."

Sarah looked over and saw Rugby finishing up his treat. It was clear he'd thoroughly enjoyed Fudderman's creation. Rugby sauntered over to a bowl of water—no doubt Misty's water—and lapped it up voraciously.

"So, Sarah," Emma said. "Did you want to go get something to drink and catch up?"

"Would love to." Emma turned to her grandfather, expectantly. "You coming?"

Larry grinned and regarded the dog that swept by his legs. "No, you girls go have fun. I have some work to do and dinner to make for us later. Besides, someone has to make sure these two don't kill each other."

Sarah hugged her grandfather once more, and Larry gave her a few pats on the back before adding, "Just make sure you're both back by dinner. I'm making something special for your first night back."

Emma and Sarah excitedly exchanged glances. Larry was known to cook like nobody's business. Both girls said in unison, "We will," before they strode out of the boutique.

Walking side by side along the street, Sarah looked into the windows of some of the storefronts, most of which weren't open yet, since the town was still technically in the latter weeks of its off-season. Soon, all of the stores would be open for business, and the little town of Cascade Cove would be a bustle of activity over the summer months.

A light breeze picked up and she could smell the salt water on the air. On the other side of the line of businesses was the boardwalk, and beyond that, the ocean. She could hear the waves lapping up onto the shoreline and wondered if the sand would be as soft as usual, or if an abundance of shells had washed up in late spring.

Chatting as they walked, Sarah saw Patricia's Tea Room off to her right. A few people were outside at tables on the sidewalk side, and she wondered how crowded the boardwalk side seating was.

"Want to go around?" Sarah asked.

Emma nodded. "You read my mind. Let's walk through—I want to see if Patricia is here."

"Isn't she always here? She owns the place, after all."

"Her granddaughter helps her now. You remember her, right?"

"Oh, yes. Nancy, isn't it? She's so nice."

"Yeah, and her grandson was working here yesterday."

Sarah scrunched her brow, thinking. "I don't think I've met him before."

"You haven't. He's an out-of-towner. From what I heard, he doesn't visit often. Probably works a lot. Sounds like someone I know," Emma said with a wink.

"Hey," Sarah said, giving her cousin a nudge.

Emma laughed and opened the door for Sarah, and waved for her to go in first.

Once inside, Sarah saw a young man behind the counter. On a huge board behind him, she saw their menu of hot and cold teas. They had flavors she'd never even known existed, fruit-infused concoctions, and baked goods and finger sandwiches to complete the ensemble.

"Hi, Danny," Emma said to the young man behind the counter. "I'll take the usual."

"The Boardwalk Banana Extravaganza," Danny said.

"You got it," Emma said with a big smile.

Sarah looked at the board. "I don't remember the Boardwalk Banana Extravaganza."

Emma turned to her. "It's semi-new and you will never forget it once you have it. Patricia came up with it last summer and it's a huge hit."

"Really? What is it?"

Danny opened his mouth, but Emma interrupted. "Okay, so they take a slice of Patricia's homemade banana bread, you know, baked with walnuts and cinnamon swirls?"

Sarah nodded. "Yeah, I love Patricia's homemade banana bread."

Emma continued, "Okay, so they take a slice of Patricia's already amazing banana bread and they grill it to perfection and top it with freshly sliced bananas. Then they add a dollop of creamy vanilla bean ice cream that is to die for, whipped cream, and then they drizzle a caramel sauce and top it with a sprinkle of candied walnuts."

Sarah's mouth dropped.

Danny chimed in, "Don't think I could've sold it better myself. And based on your face, I think I'll just make that two orders of the Boardwalk Banana Extravaganza."

Sarah nodded. "Yes, please."

"And would you like the cream tea?"

"Can't have the Banana Extravaganza without Patricia's cream tea, now, could we?" Emma said with a chuckle.

"I guess not. By the way," Danny turned to Sarah, "I didn't catch your name."

"Sarah."

Danny smiled, repeating her name back to her. "I don't think I've seen you around before."

"She's my cousin," Emma said. "Came to visit for a couple of weeks, just like you."

"Ah, I see," he said. "Nice to meet you."

"Likewise," Sarah said with a smile.

"Well then, you can have a seat and I'll bring your order over to you." He made a show of getting their tea and dessert ready.

"We'll be on the boardwalk side," Emma said to the young man. Danny nodded without taking his eyes off of what he was doing.

Opening the door, Sarah saw the waves crashing down on the velvet sand. She smiled when she saw the idyllic beach she'd been excited to enjoy. It would surely calm her nerves.

Sarah's smile drifted from her face when she looked off in the distance. Dark, brooding clouds lingered above the horizon.

Emma took a seat near a woman wearing a brimmed hat who was sitting alone, sipping tea.

Still standing, Sarah caught movement to the left a long way down the beach, near the pier that ran a hundred yards or so into the ocean. The pier's thick pillars were being ravaged by the choppy waves. There were a few men on the beach near the pier. They were wearing uniforms.

"Police officers?" Sarah muttered. "Wonder what's going on…"

"Storm's coming," Emma said.

"Looks like it," Sarah said, louder this time. She kept her gaze fixed on the activity near the pier as a cool breeze whipped past her exposed arms. Goosebumps quickly appeared, and she felt a chill as she stared, her curiosity getting the better of her.

CHAPTER 2

"Sarah?" Emma said. "Earth to Sarah."

The loud clatter of a cup against a saucer broke Sarah from her trance. She looked down at her cousin, feeling her heartrate pick up slightly. In her daze, she'd apparently missed the fact that their tea and dessert had been delivered to the table.

"Try some," Emma said, picking up her cup of tea. After taking a sip, she returned the cup to its saucer, a blissful smile on her face.

Sarah sat down and regarded the spread of tea and the two orders of Banana Extravaganza that sat between her and her cousin. She felt the smooth side of the fine china to test the tea's temperature. Before she could pick up her cup, she heard a voice off to her right.

"Good afternoon, Emma," said the woman in the brimmed hat.

"Marigold," Emma said, her voice emotionless.

"Another beautiful day in the Cove," Marigold said, her southern accent heavy. Sarah eyed the woman, envious of her loosely curled strawberry-blonde hair that waved out from the summer hat. She wore a beautiful floral dress with elegant shoes. She took a sip of her tea and gently set the cup in its saucer with no more than a barely-audible *clink*. Then she lifted the fine cloth napkin that had laid across her lap, and raised it to her ruby-red lips, dabbing softly. "So, who's your friend? Have we met before?"

"This is Sarah," Emma said. "She's my cousin. Lives up north, in New York City."

"Pleasure to meet you, Sarah," Marigold said, putting a hand out to shake Sarah's.

Sarah shook her hand. "The pleasure's mine. I think we've met before…"

"Perhaps you've stopped into my wine shop? Or seen me around town?"

"Oh, that's right. I love Dunham Vineyards' wine."

Marigold beamed. "Thank you, kindly."

"How are things going with the vineyard?" Emma asked, picking up her fork and puncturing through the soft, crisp banana bread as her knife slid down through the ice cream like butter. She cut a big piece and shoveled it into her mouth, looking ready to devour the entire dessert in seconds.

Marigold took another sip of her tea and smiled, though Sarah could tell the smile was plastic. What history did these two have?

"Going well, thanks for asking."

"I heard you had a soil issue," Emma said, looking up to catch Marigold's reaction. "What was it? Contamination?" Emma cocked her head to the side, waiting for an answer.

Marigold cleared her throat and let out a nervous chuckle, shaking her head. Sarah could tell she was trying to remain calm. Obviously, something was going on at the vineyard and Emma had struck a nerve.

Sarah eyed Emma, giving her a look that telegraphed, "Be nice." Then Sarah turned to Marigold. "Hey, you wouldn't happen to know what's going on by the pier?"

"You two haven't heard about John Jacobs?" Marigold asked.

Emma looked back at Marigold. "No, what's going on with Old Man Jacobs?"

"Well, apparently, he had a bit of an accident."

"Accident? What happened?"

Marigold took another sip of her tea, looking a bit

uneasy. "Well," she said, dabbing one side of her mouth with her napkin, then the other.

Sarah leaned forward in her chair.

Marigold stared down at her tea. "To put it bluntly, Mr. Jacobs drowned."

Sarah's eyes widened. "Drowned?"

"I'm afraid so," Marigold said, lips pursed.

"When did this happen?"

"Listen, I should be going," Marigold said, lifting her napkin, this time to her eyes. Sarah could see they were now puffy, slightly red. "I have an appointment, and I don't wish to be late."

Marigold rose from her chair, leaving her empty tea cup for Danny to retrieve.

"Good day, ladies," Marigold said, sweeping past them, almost running into a handsome, uniformed man.

"Hi, ma'am," the officer said to Marigold.

"Hello there, Adam," she said, then stepped away, going through the main tea room.

Sarah watched the officer approach them, and he smiled in recognition. Adam Dunkin. He was carrying a plate with a couple of Patricia's famous mini lemon meringue tarts, and he set it down on one of the adjacent tables. He stepped toward them. "Well, if it isn't Sarah Shores."

"Hey, Adam," Sarah said, rising from her seat. She

hugged the man, feeling his muscular body during their brief embrace.

He tipped his hat at Emma. "You didn't say Sarah was coming to town this soon."

"We didn't have any snow days this year," Sarah said. She saw the man smiling fondly at her, the same smile that had adorned that face the first time she ever saw it. He was just a summer-time companion, back then. Someone who tagged along on her and Emma's escapades, helping them cause trouble around town. Now, he was the one nipping trouble in the bud.

"Still teaching?" Adam asked.

"Yeah, fifth year."

"Like it?"

Sarah shrugged. "It's a job. The kids can be a bit much."

"How's that?"

"I don't know. I guess sometimes I feel more like a case worker."

Sarah heard a man yell behind her, off in the direction of the pier. Another man called back, his words garbled by the growing winds. Sarah turned around, but the men were too far away for her to see any recognizable features.

She turned back to Adam and asked, "What's going on over there?"

"They're looking into a recent drowning."

Sarah's body tensed. "Was it…uh, Mr. Jacobs?"

Adam nodded. "Yeah, how did you know?"

Emma said, "You know how gossip flocks around here."

Adam looked at Emma for a moment, then turned his attention back to Sarah. "Well, it isn't just gossip this time. Some fishermen reported it this morning. We think it happened sometime last night."

"How did he drown?"

Adam looked over at the pier. His colleagues were clearly out of earshot, but Sarah could tell he was apprehensive about giving her any information about what had happened.

"Sorry," she said, feeling her face flush at the error.

Adam flashed her a smile, eyes set on hers. He lowered his voice and said, "Don't be sorry. All I can say now is that it's looking like an accidental drowning."

"Oh."

A two-way radio clipped to Adam's belt squawked, though Sarah couldn't make out any of what was said.

"Oh, I'm being summoned, apparently. No such thing as a break," Adam said, grabbing his plate and taking a bite of the delicate pastry. Sarah mused at the idea of such a strong man eating such a dainty dessert. But how could he not? Patricia's desserts were magical.

"Nice to see you," Sarah said.

"You, as well. How long will you be in town?"

"Two weeks," Sarah said. "We'll have to play catch-up."

"You'll be at Larry's shop later, I assume?"

Sarah nodded.

"Okay," Adam said. "I'll stop by later."

They said their goodbyes, and she watched Adam take another large bite out of the pastry, stepping back into the tea shop. She saw him return his plate to Danny, and head through to the street, where his police cruiser was likely parked.

Sarah and Emma finished their food and drinks and chatted about subjects not related to accidental drownings, but Sarah couldn't shake the thought of it.

After they finished up at Patricia's Tea Room, they said their goodbyes to Danny and headed back to their grandfather's boutique.

Side by side, they walked in silence. Normally, Emma was as chatty as a wren—something was nagging at her cousin.

"Everything okay?" Sarah asked.

"Yeah."

They reached their grandfather's shop and entered. Inside, Larry looked frazzled as Rugby galloped around the cat, almost knocking over the display of nicely organized bandanas and then almost knocking over a glass jar of tags. Larry rushed over and caught it before it tipped over. "Rugby!"

Sarah sighed and grabbed Rugby. "Hey, boy. Calm down."

Rugby sat next to Sarah's feet and panted, looking up at everyone.

"I'm sorry, Grandpa. Is Rugby too much for you?" Sarah asked.

"Of course not," Larry said, adjusting the bandana display. Sarah could tell when her grandfather was feigning enthusiasm, and this was one of those moments.

Sarah stepped toward the counter and spotted Rugby's leash. "He's been cooped up in the car for a long time, now acting like a bull in a china shop here."

"Good thing we don't have porcelain tea sets here," Larry said, raking his thin fingers through his hair. He gave Sarah a smile and peered around, as if looking to see if Rugby had knocked anything else over.

Her mind drifted back to tea sets, and she thought of her conversations back at Patricia's Tea Room.

Sarah regarded her grandfather. "Say, did you hear what happened to Mr. Jacobs?"

"No, what happened?"

"He drowned…" Emma started.

Larry looked crestfallen upon hearing the news.

Emma continued, "...which is really strange."

"I'll say," Larry said.

"What?" Sarah asked. "What's so strange about Mr. Jacobs drowning? We have accidental drownings here at the Cove. It's unfortunate, but it happens..."

"I thought everyone knew about the running joke about John Jacobs," Larry said.

"C'mon," Sarah said in a huff. "Out with it."

"About how odd it is he lives so close to the ocean," Larry said.

"He never goes out to the pier," Emma said. "You don't remember?"

Just then, Sarah remembered what everyone in Cascade Cove already knew.

"That's right," she said. "Mr. Jacobs is deathly afraid of the water."

CHAPTER 3

"That's exactly right," Larry said, looking more serious than Sarah had seen him in a long time. "Jacobs is never seen close to the water, not even on the sand. The farthest he goes out is when he's walking along the boardwalk."

Sarah's brow furrowed. So that was probably the key detail that must've been nagging at Emma on their walk back from the tea shop.

Now, Sarah was filled with the same puzzled thoughts.

She wondered how on Earth Mr. Jacobs drowned if he never went in the water, much less near it.

"But wait," Sarah said, "why would he live in Cascade Cove, especially so close to the ocean, if he's that afraid of the water?"

"It's his home," Larry said. "His family has roots that run deep here, and he has told me numerous times how he loves the smell of salt water."

Sarah's eyes grew wide. "So, do you think…" Sarah started.

"Maybe it wasn't an accident," Emma chimed in.

"Always jumping to conclusions," Larry said, shaking his head. "I'm sure there's a perfectly reasonable explanation for how a man who was afraid of water ended up in the water."

"Yeah, someone put him there," Emma said.

"Then who?" Larry said, challenging her.

Emma shrugged. "I don't know."

Sarah took a deep breath and grabbed Rugby's leash. "Grandpa's right, there's probably a good explanation. There usually is."

The sound of the collar and leash swinging in her hand was all it took for Rugby to come rushing toward her. Off in the distance, Misty purred, probably settled in one of her secret sleeping spots on a top shelf somewhere in the boutique.

"I don't buy it," Emma said, crossing her arms. Her face was scrunched up in a scowl. "So, you think a man who was deathly afraid of the water decided one day, 'You know what, I feel like going for a dip'?"

"There's got to be a logical explanation. That's all I'm saying," Larry said.

"I'm going to take Rugby," Sarah cut in. "Anyone want to go along?"

"We're still open," Larry said, "so count me out."

Emma shook her head, still looking perturbed. "I need to finish up in the office. Orders need to go out today, so we get fully stocked for when the floodgates open and the tourists flock in."

"Okay," Sarah said, putting Rugby's collar on him.

"Is your car open?" Larry asked.

"Why?"

"Figured I could get your luggage upstairs before the rain hits."

"Thanks, but I can do it quick. Is your apartment unlocked?" she asked, fishing her keys out of her pocket. "Stay here, Rugby."

"Should be," Larry said. "And you brought the shirts, right?"

"Sweaters, yeah. A whole box of them," Sarah said, smiling. Her homemade knitted dog sweaters were always a hit with the tourists, especially those who lived in the northern states. Though some were lightweight enough for a cool summer evening, most were ideal for keeping a dog warm during the winter months in other regions.

"Great," Larry said. "Bring them in here so I can make sure they're on display; prominently, of course."

"Will do."

Rugby let out a groan of disappointment as Sarah rushed out the door.

Out at her car, she grabbed her things, and took them up the stairs to her Grandpa's apartment above the boutique.

She let herself into his apartment. The smell of a mid-day meal lingered in the air, though the kitchen showed no signs of any mess left behind. Larry was quite the efficient chef, able to simultaneously cook and clean up. His cooking was equally as impressive as his wife's brownies, and Sarah let out a sigh at the fact that she might miss seeing her globetrotting grandmother during her visit.

Putting her things down in one corner of the carpeted living room, she spotted pictures on the wall. She went up to the pictures and smiled. There, she saw her grandma and grandpa flanking her and Emma when they were just kids.

"Good times," she said, studying the picture. That was the summer she'd first met Adam, she remembered.

Sarah stepped out of the apartment. She'd have to spend some time looking over old pictures later, and made a mental note to ask her grandpa about any old photo albums or scrapbooks they had lying around—her grandma was famous for her scrapbooks, so there was bound to be one somewhere.

She made her way down the steps and back out to her car to grab the dog sweaters from her trunk. She carried the medium-sized box into the store and placed it behind the counter.

Rugby was waiting patiently by Larry's side as he stocked a shelf, using his prized Garvey price gun to put neon green, rectangular stickers on fresh stock. "I'm excited to see what kind of dog-shirt designs you have this year," Larry said. "I'll take some pictures to put them on the web site."

"How are mail-order sales going?"

"Better than off-season sales in the store," Larry said, finishing up stocking a shelf. "Emma is working on updating our website so we can do sales online. Says it will be easier." He turned and pointed at Sarah, holding the price gun in the other hand. "I have some money for you."

"I told you to keep it."

Larry waved dismissively at her. "No, no," he said. "You've got to get paid for your work."

"But I want to make sure you're okay."

Larry smiled. "I appreciate that, Sarah, but your grandma and I are fine."

"But—"

"Besides," Larry cut in, "fair is fair. I'll cut you a check later."

"Okay," she said, not wanting to argue with her grandfather further. The truth was, she knitted the sweaters for fun while watching TV at night, so in her mind, her only cost was materials. She would have rather let her grandparents keep the money, if only to help keep their boutique up and running.

"You better hurry up and go for your walk before the rains come."

"Right."

Sarah grabbed Rugby's leash, and he looked up, hopeful.

"Let's go, boy," she said, and they strode out of the shop together, plenty of slack in the leash, as usual.

Outside, the wind grew stronger. Sarah knew the walk would be brief as a result of the incoming storm.

She hurried past Patricia's Tea Room and up along the main road of Cascade Cove. On her left, she saw the bowling alley, closed for the season. She spotted the ice cream shop, a favorite hangout for the locals. Through the windows, she noticed a couple of employees cleaning up, getting ready to close for the evening.

Rugby still walking in lockstep with her, Sarah saw the bakery.

"Want to go into Fudderman's, boy?" There were never enough baked goods in Cascade Cove with the tourists flooding all of the stores during the summertime. And each bakery had their own special item that was a hit. Fudderman's was his cakes and chocolates.

Rugby galloped toward the large glass doors of the lit-up bakery, an indication that he was more than eager to see Henry Fudderman.

Through the door they went, and a man behind the counter beamed a smile through his white beard.

"Miss Sarah!"

"Hey there, Mr. Fudderman."

"Oh, please...call me Henry."

Henry Fudderman was around Larry's age, his hair now white as a fresh blanket of snow. Whatever part of his face one could see above his beard was flushed red; she would understand if someone mistook him for Kris Kringle. His voice boomed, echoing inside the quaint bakery. Looking around, she saw that none of the tables were occupied.

"Yeah, been slow so far," Henry said, noticing her looking around at the vacant seating area.

"It'll pick up," she said.

"Oh, let me get something for your furry friend." Henry ducked down behind the counter, and in a flash, was back up holding a treat in his hand. "I bet he's never had anything as scrumptious as this."

Henry squeezed between an opening in the counter and handed Rugby the treat. Rugby gobbled up the treat in one fell swoop and Sarah giggled.

"Not the first time," she said.

"Oh, that's right. Your Grandpa Larry probably gave him one already. Sorry, I should have asked."

"No, it's okay."

"So, did you want one of my famous Fudder Cream Donuts? Or perhaps a Cascade Cruller?"

"Is the first one like a Boston Cream?"

"Better."

"I'll take one of those."

"Anything else?"

"Hmm," Sarah said, eyeing the menu, written behind the old man in different colored chalks. "What's that Boardwalk Fudge Cake all about?"

"Ah, yes. The Boardwalk Fudge Cake. It's a six-inch, four-layer chocolate cake filled with chocolate mousse and cubes of homemade chocolate fudge. It's finished with even more chocolate mousse, and as you can see," Henry said, pointing to a delicious-looking cake in the main display case, "it's topped with even more chocolate cubes."

Sarah gazed at the marvel, noting the chocolate drip

down along the side of the cake. She looked around at the other cakes on display, unsure of which to choose.

"I think I'll go with the Boardwalk Fudge Cake."

"A surprise for your grandpa?"

"Yeah, Grandma's out of town, so…"

"Off on another trip, is she?"

"Yeah. Cruising around the world."

With plastic-gloved hands, Henry put her desired cake in a fancy box and then into an equally fancy bag. Then he got one of the Fudder Cream Donuts and asked, "Did you want to eat this one here, or should I wrap it up to go?"

"I'll eat it here," she said.

Henry placed the donut on a plate and set it on the counter. Sarah paid for the baked goods, and grabbed the plate and the bag containing the cake. She sauntered over to one of the many empty tables and took a seat.

Henry stood behind the counter, still beaming. "It is so good to see you again," he said. "I remember when you were a young tyke. You used to have pigtails and a fancy bow. I feel like that was yesterday."

Sarah took a bite of donut, and chewed it slowly, enjoying the texture and sweet flavor. "This is as good as I remember it," she muttered.

"Glad you're enjoying it," Henry said. "And I

remember when you were a kid, me and Larry would take you fishing on the pier. Such fun!"

She stopped chewing her donut and felt her chest tighten. She thought back to the police officers at the pier. What she'd learned from Marigold Dunham and Adam Dunkin.

Looking over at Henry, she saw he was still smiling. Did he not know about John Jacobs? Was he cloistered in his bakery without enough foot traffic to allow for the latest gossip to hit his ears?

Sarah considered not saying anything, but the curiosity inside her was welling up, ready to explode.

Before she could ask, Henry said, "What troubles you?"

"Didn't you hear about John Jacobs?"

Henry shook his head. "I've been out of town the past few days, just got in this morning. Didn't hear the latest Jacobs gossip. What's that rascal getting mixed up into this time? Can't be worse than last week's debacle."

"What do you mean?"

"I guess you don't know about the trouble he's been causing around town, during the off-season, no less."

"You still lost me."

"Well, he owns a lot of property in the area. Landlord to many of the small businesses. Not your grandpa, of course—Larry is lucky to own his building. But not all of us can be that lucky. Jacobs is my landlord, among many others. He's raised the rent twenty percent this year, on top of last year's increase."

"That's awful."

"Yeah," Henry said. "Patricia is taking it harder than most of us. Last week, I was over there getting tea and she said she'd clobber him over the head with her cane next chance she got. Usually she's sweet, and just joking, but she sounded like she was serious."

"And you think her threat was over the rent increase?"

"Yeah, I assume it was that. But it wasn't until he insulted her infamous oatmeal cookies, the very first treat she served alongside her teas that took her business to the next level, that she made the threat."

Sarah's eyes went wide. "What did he say?"

"That her cookie was a bit too dry for his taste." Henry Fudderman shook his head. "She takes a lot of pride in everything she makes in that shop. I can relate, but I don't think I would ever threaten harm on anyone if they insulted my cakes."

Sarah set the uneaten half of her donut on the plate, feeling her jaw drop slightly.

Henry's beaming smile was nowhere to be found. His tone now serious, he asked, "What's the matter, dear? You look like you've seen a ghost."

CHAPTER 4

*S*arah grabbed the remaining half of her uneaten donut and took a large bite, giving her a much-needed moment to think over her response.

Chewing, she saw the look on Henry Fudderman's face.

A look of worry.

Did she want to be the one to break this news to him?

He'd find out about John Jacobs' death eventually—it didn't have to be through her, though.

To Sarah, Henry Fudderman was the wonderful old man who was the only person she knew who could bake as well as Grandma. Kind and sweet—a gentle soul. She wasn't sure how he would take the news.

Swallowing the delicious piece of donut, she made

her decision about how to reply.

"I'm fine, really," she said, forcing a smile.

"Are you sure? You know you can tell me anything."

Outside, she could hear the wind thumping against the glass windows of the bakery. Soon, sheets of rain would be pounding the pavement, making her walk back to her grandpa's eventful.

"I should get back before it starts to pour," she said, then finished her donut.

Henry nodded, and Sarah saw a hint of a smile appear. "Yeah. You don't have long till the heavens open up. Tell your grandpa to stop by soon. He's right down the street, but we never run into each other."

"He's been busy getting ready for the tourists."

"Same here. Well, Miss Sarah, have a nice night. Stay dry."

Sarah grabbed the bagged cake and Rugby's leash, and left the bakery, waving to Henry Fudderman as she went. Soon, the old man would catch wind of the recent events, but she was glad she wasn't the one to break the news, even if Henry Fudderman considered John Jacobs a "rascal."

"Let's get back to Grandpa's," Sarah said, walking down the street. The ice cream shop employees were getting in their cars, driving away for the night. Other than them, the street was vacant.

Once their cars were out of sight, Sarah surveyed the main strip. Cascade Cove looked like a ghost town.

Motion off to her right caught her eye.

Shadows filled the sidewalk on the other side of the street, near a barbershop.

Sarah froze and watched, but saw nothing.

She and Rugby continued on. Soon, they'd be back at Grandpa's boutique and—

A sound behind her caught her attention.

She whipped around and heard Rugby growl lightly. "Easy, boy."

Perhaps it was the wind, she thought.

Or perhaps it was something else…

She turned back around and continued along.

There it was again—that same noise. A metallic clinking sound.

Before she could turn around again to rush back to the safety of her grandpa's place, she saw the source of the sound.

Out of the shadows, a small dog strode toward her, a tag clinking against a part of its collar as he went.

"What are you doing out here?" Sarah said, her voice soft and soothing.

Rugby's tail wagged at the sight of a potential play-pal. He sat obediently without Sarah's command, though she was about to issue it.

"Reading my mind again, boy?"

Rugby looked up, happy as ever.

The small dog approached them, unafraid. She was familiar with the breed—it was a corgi, its golden hair trimmed short, like it had been recently groomed, though his paw looked dirty. Its ears were perked up, alert.

"What's that hanging out of your mouth?"

Sarah crouched down and reached out her hand, her palm faced upward, showing she meant no harm.

The dog came closer and let the object he was holding in his mouth fall into her hand, as if he were delivering it to her. She looked at it, practically studying it. It seemed to be some sort of antique locket necklace with a tree-like symbol inscribed on it. While still crouched down, she could see the corgi's tag glimmering. On it, she saw an engraved name: WINSTON.

"Hi, Winston. Nice to meet you." She looked around. "Where are your owners?"

The first raindrops of the night struck the pavement, and Sarah knew that soon, a torrential downpour would ensue.

Winston sat and let out a small whimper.

Sarah sighed and looked up at the sky. Thunder cracked loudly and she looked back at the small corgi.

"C'mon, Winston," she said, patting her leg. "You can't be out here in the rain at night."

The dog started following her, and she led the way, looking over her shoulder every dozen steps to ensure the corgi was still hot on her trail.

A flash of lightning followed by another loud *crack* startled her, but both dogs racing toward the boutique with her were unperturbed. Off in the distance, beyond her grandpa's place, she saw a man in black dashing from a parked car and into a neighboring building. She wondered if the man lived in the upstairs apartment of the neighboring Bait and Tackle store.

The man was quickly out of sight, and Sarah didn't pay it a second mind.

She had an important mission, one she knew might soon fail: stay dry.

The sky opened, and the water hitting the concrete sounded like a thousand miniature waves lapping up to shore. Ahead, she saw Larry standing at the open door to the boutique, waving her on.

"Hurry!"

In the next moment, she, Rugby, and Winston were inside the boutique, the sound of rain growing louder, even as the glass door swept closed.

"Look at you," Larry said, smirking. "Another minute out there, and you'd be completely soaked."

Sarah felt the weight of the wet clothes and knew it could've been worse. Though her hair was dripping, she felt exhilarated.

"Why don't you go up to get a change of...wait a minute," Larry said, looking at the corgi. "Who's this fella?"

"That's Winston."

Larry scratched his head. "Don't you think one dog is enough? I know you rescued Rugby, but—"

"He followed me home," Sarah said.

"Where's his owner?"

"I don't know, but I couldn't just leave him out there. And it's not the best time to see if there's anyone looking for him. It's a mess out there."

"Hmm."

"Yeah, you're telling me."

Misty swept by Winston, and the corgi dodged him the same way Rugby always had.

"Looks like it's two to one, now, Misty," Larry said.

Sarah chuckled. "Even at two-to-one, that evil cat still outnumbers them."

Larry grabbed his chest and raised his eyebrows. "Evil? After all she's done for you..."

"Grandpa, she's a grumpy old cat and—"

"I guess you're not getting brownies after this display," Larry said, with a wink.

"Then I guess you're not getting what's in this bag."

Larry stepped closer, peering down at the bag as if he were expecting the top to be open so he could see right in. "What's in there? Looks like a Fudderman bag."

"A Boardwalk Fudge Cake," Sarah said, holding the bag closer.

Larry gasped. "You've found my weakness!"

Sarah laughed and said, "Want to spoil our dinners?"

Emma came out from the back office, her eyes bloodshot from working on putting an order together.

"Did you call Bob yet, Grandpa?"

"The handyman? Why would I call him?"

Emma let out a heavy breath. "You asked me to remind you to call him to fix the light above the bowtie display."

"Oh yes, that's right."

"Bowties?" Sarah asked.

"Yeah, it's new," Emma said. "We have them for cats and dogs. Tried to get Misty to wear one to model for our customers, but she won't have it."

Larry laughed. "That's an understatement." He turned to Emma, pointing at the bag in Sarah's hand. "So, Sarah brought cake."

Emma shrugged but said nothing.

"Suit yourself," Larry said, then winked at Sarah again. "More for us."

✿

Upstairs, Sarah changed into dry clothing and came out to the living room to see Rugby, Winston, and Misty rushing around. It was clear the two dogs were playing, though Sarah couldn't tell if Misty was also playing or if she was harassing her canine counterparts, as usual.

Emma stood with arms crossed, looking at the three animals. She looked up at Sarah and shook her head. "You're not here more than ten hours and somehow you doubled the amount of dogs you have."

"He's not mine."

"Uh-huh."

"He's not."

"Where did you get him?"

"She found him," Larry said from the kitchen. Sarah could smell the plate of chocolate chip brownies he was holding. "Fresh out of the oven. Eat up, girls."

"No dinner?" Emma asked.

Larry looked over to Sarah. "Get the cake out."

Emma sighed. "Grandma leaves, and you're like a kid again, eating sweets for dinner."

"You know how to cook," Larry said to Emma, putting the plate of steaming brownies on the kitchen table.

"I'm not the chef around here," she said. "You are."

"I'm taking the night off," he said, picking up a brownie and taking a copious bite. Chewing it, he opened up the refrigerator and grabbed a container of milk. "Anyone else want some milk?"

"I'll take some," Sarah said, taking a seat at the dining room table. She picked up a brownie and took a bite. Being at her grandparents' place always meant lots of food, but she hadn't had this many sweets in a long time.

Emma sat across from her, took one look at the brownies, and said, "Oh, what the heck." She grabbed a brownie and took a bite, like she'd been without chocolate for a decade.

Larry brought over three glasses of milk and set them down. Sarah took a sip, feeling the cold beverage hit her tongue.

"What's that?" Emma asked.

Sarah took another bite of brownie. "What?"

"That thing around your neck. Did you just buy that?"

Sarah lifted her hand and felt the antique locket that was in front of her chest, hanging from the necklace. She saw Winston in her peripherals, then fixed her gaze on Emma. "Funny thing about this locket. Winston gave it to me."

CHAPTER 5

"Who's Winston?" Emma asked. "New boyfriend, or—"

Sarah nearly choked on her milk, struggling to keep it from going out her nose and onto the plate of chocolate chip brownies in between her and her cousin.

"Winston's this fella," Larry said, pointing down at the corgi that continued to play with Rugby and Misty.

"Wait, I'm confused," Emma said.

"Winston had this wooden, antique locket hanging from his mouth when I found him, like he'd picked it up somewhere."

Larry came over to the table and sat down. "You didn't tell me about that."

"Didn't have time to," Sarah said. "You were too busy eyeing up my cake."

"Oh yes," Larry said, getting up abruptly. "I forgot to put out the cake. Can't forget the main course."

Emma rolled her eyes.

"The odd thing about it," Sarah said, "is it's the heaviest locket I've ever felt. And it has a tree engraved on the front of it, with roots and all."

"Really? Can I see it?" Emma held out her hand, waiting for the necklace.

Sarah took it from around her neck and handed it over to her cousin.

"Well it's old, so they probably used real wood or something and that's why it feels so heavy. They didn't use anything cheap back then."

"Back when?" Sarah asked.

"I don't know," Emma said, inspecting it. "Wow, this tree is very intricate. Looks like the Tree of Life, almost. Wonder where he found it?" Emma said, pushing her thumbnails into the side of it, trying to pry it apart.

"What are you doing?" Sarah said.

"Trying to open it. Might give us a clue to who Winston belongs to."

"Good point."

Emma let out a small grunt as she struggled to open it, to no avail. "It won't open," she said in frustration.

Sarah took the necklace back and looked at it. There

were slits on either side, suggesting it could open. But upon further inspection, she said, "There are no hinges."

"Try opening it from the bottom."

Sarah tried. "Nope, I don't think it opens. Probably just glued two slats of wood together. It's old."

"Yeah, that it is," Emma said, then drank the rest of her milk.

"It's a pendant, then," Larry said. Carrying over the container of milk, he poured her a second glass before she could tell him she didn't want any more.

"So, looks like you lucked out today," Emma said. "A new antique locket—"

"Pendant," Larry said.

Emma corrected herself, "A new antique pendant, a new dog—"

"I'm not keeping Winston. His owners are probably worried sick about him. I'm putting up flyers tomorrow."

"So how was Henry Fudderman when you saw him?" Larry asked.

"Good, but apparently he doesn't know about John Jacobs yet."

"He never liked him much anyway."

"I heard."

"Oh yeah?"

"Henry Fudderman said John Jacobs is his landlord—"

"Right, right," Larry said, bringing the cake to the table. He sliced a piece and put it on a plate, giving it to Emma. "Here, dear."

Emma looked down at the cake, uninterested. Then she looked at Sarah. "His landlord?"

"Yeah, and Jacobs raised the rent for all of his tenants this year, including Henry Fudderman. Twenty percent —can you believe that?"

Emma's eyes lit up, a mischievous grin fixed on her face.

"What are you smiling about?" Sarah asked.

"Don't you see?" Emma said. "John Jacobs was afraid of water. He raises the rent for his tenants. Next thing you know, he's dead. And you just said Henry Fudderman didn't like him much and—"

"Henry didn't even know about Jacobs' drowning."

Emma leaned forward, placing both elbows on the table, still ignoring her piece of cake. "Could be a ruse."

"What do you mean, a ruse?"

"Fudderman's trying to trick you."

Sarah shook her head. "You're crazy. Henry had no idea about what happened to Jacobs—"

"How do you know?"

"If you'd let me finish, I was going to say he had no

idea because he was out of town. Just got back this morning, in fact. Jacobs drowned last night."

"Was *murdered* last night," Emma corrected.

"Jumping to conclusions again," Larry chimed in.

Emma turned to her grandpa. "No."

"Yeah, you are. He told me about his nephew's graduation party he was planning to attend out of town. I remember him saying the event was, let's see…" Larry looked at a calendar on his refrigerator. "Yesterday evening."

"Solid alibi," Sarah said.

"Grandpa," Emma pleaded, "he could have just told you that so he has a solid alibi."

"His bakery was closed," Larry said. "And his car was gone. I even saw a picture today that Henry texted to me." Larry pulled out his phone and quickly brought up the picture. "Boy's taller than Henry now. And roughly fifty people were at the party and would have seen him."

Sarah smiled. "That's an iron-clad alibi if I've ever heard one."

Emma slumped in her chair.

"Still…" Sarah started, then took her fork to her small piece of brownie, saving the cake for last.

Emma sat up. "Go on…"

"Well, I was just thinking about what Henry Fudderman said."

"About?"

"About what Patricia said."

"Oh, how's Patty doing?" Larry asked.

Sarah ignored her grandpa. "As you might know, she's a tenant of John Jacobs—"

"Oh yeah, she is," said Larry, face now buried in the fridge.

"—and last week, Henry was at her Tea Room and overheard her say that she'd clobber Jacobs over the head with her cane next chance she got."

"Because of the rent increase?" Emma asked.

"That, and I heard he also insulted her cookies. Said they were a bit too dry for his taste."

"She can be a bit defensive when it comes to harsh critiques of her baked goods or tea. But she's a sweetheart," Larry said, closing the refrigerator.

"It's a facade," Emma said.

"Normally, I'd disagree with you," Sarah said, "but she has a solid motive, and unlike Henry Fudderman, no alibi."

"Not that you know of," Larry said.

"Of course."

"How do you know about all this stuff, anyway? Alibis and motives and the like?"

"Maybe from hanging around Adam every summer."

Larry nodded. "Right."

"Anyway," Sarah said to no one in particular, "we should go talk to Patricia tomorrow."

In the middle of eating another brownie, Larry stopped abruptly. "I don't think you should."

"Why not?"

"Let the police do their jobs. As far as we know, it was an accident. That's what everyone has been saying."

Sarah considered what her grandpa said. Perhaps she was jumping the gun, most likely being egged on by her cousin. Still, the whole thing seemed suspicious. Something was going on, and she wanted to get to the bottom of it. She decided to compromise, not wanting to rock the boat too much.

"Fine," Sarah said. "I'll call Adam tomorrow and tell him what I heard. Then I'll leave this whole thing alone."

"Sarah, c'mon," Emma said. "The police will let the perp slip right through their fingers..."

"Listen to your cousin," Larry said to Emma. "Focus on finding Winston's rightful owners, and let the police handle the serious matters."

Sarah noted Larry's unusually serious tone coming out again. She didn't like this side of her grandpa—preferring his whimsical side—but in this case, she was glad for the backup.

Emma picked up her fork, finally taking a bite of her soft chocolate chip brownie. "Well, one thing I know for sure is that we are all going to have belly aches tonight."

"At least our belly aches won't be a mystery," Sarah said with a chuckle. Though, she couldn't help but let what they had been talking about swirl around in her mind. Off to her left, Rugby, Winston, and Misty continued to play, ignorant to what was transpiring in the human world.

Of course, the John Jacobs incident was likely an accident, and the idea of Patricia Greensmith murdering him was absurd.

Sarah thought back to all of the other crazy things she heard in her life that turned out to be true. It was possible that this was one of them.

The next day, Sarah sat on a stool behind the counter of the boutique, finishing up a dog sweater she'd been knitting and waiting for the morning's first customer to come in. Bored, she opened her laptop and scanned the websites of small, family-run vendors in pursuit of the next hot item to stock, while Rugby and Winston lightly snored behind her.

Rugby seemed to take a great liking to Winston from the start and the two seemed to get along well. They both slept in her room the night before without any fuss, and the morning went smoothly as they both ate breakfast together. The only one who seemed to oppose it was Misty, her cousin's Persian cat. But Sarah made it a point to tell Winston not to take it personally. Misty wasn't much of a dog lover, and she spent most of the morning up in her cozy spot on the shelf, overlooking the boutique.

Meanwhile, in the back office, her grandpa and Emma worked on finalizing the order she'd worked on the previous day. She had promised to cover the shop for two hours while they completed that task, then she'd take Rugby and Winston out on the town, mainly to try to track down Winston's owner. She already had flyers printed out, ready to go.

The bell above the entrance jingled, and Sarah looked up to see a stocky man in overalls walking in.

Winston woke up and gave a little growl.

"Winston, no. That's not nice." Sarah turned her attention to the man. "I'm sorry about that, sir, I just found him yesterday wandering alone, and he isn't used to the sounds here and people coming in and out of the store yet. Can I help you?"

"Is Larry here?"

"Yeah, let me get him."

Back in the office, Sarah let her grandpa know

someone was here to talk to him. He walked out with her and stepped up to shake the man's hand.

"Hey, Bob. Thanks for coming out on such short notice," Larry said to the man, who Sarah figured was the handyman.

The man grabbed his tools and followed Larry to the other side of the boutique, in the back, to fix whatever needed fixing. Above her paygrade, she mused.

She stared out into the empty boutique, praying for customers, much like farmers would pray for rain.

She let out a sigh and looked at the time displayed on the righthand corner of her laptop's screen. Seeing the time, she let out another sigh. Another hour to go...

Her eyes opened wider when she had a flash of realization. She forgot to call Adam Dunkin to give him the hearsay from Henry Fudderman about Patricia Greensmith. Surely, he would laugh at the notion of the little old lady doing such a thing, though she felt the responsibility to pass on such information to the authorities, and Adam was her direct line to the fine men and women who served and protected the Cove and its occupants.

She reached into her pocket to retrieve her cell phone. When she pressed a button on the side of the device, she saw that she'd missed a call from Adam.

Apparently, she'd forgotten to take her phone off its silent mode.

"Looks like he left a message."

She accessed her phone's voicemail and listened to Adam's message.

"Hi, Sarah, it's Adam. Just calling to give you an update on what we talked about yesterday. Give me a call back when you get this."

Sarah immediately dialed Adam and waited.

On the third ring, she expected to hit voicemail at any moment.

"Hello?" came the voice.

They said their hellos and Adam got right to the point: "Listen, Sarah. I'm still at work now, so I don't think I can talk…"

"Want me to call you later?"

Adam's voice was a bit quieter as he continued, "Here's the thing, I learned more about that thing we were talking about yesterday."

"Okay, what is it?"

"Autopsy came back. There was a bump on the back of his head."

"A bump?" Sarah nearly dropped the phone. Her mind immediately fixated on the little old lady and her cane.

What if…

"Yeah," Adam said, interrupting her thoughts. His voice was barely a whisper. He must've been afraid someone would overhear him, though she was uncertain why he would risk getting in trouble giving her this info. They went back a long way, and she had a feeling he might've had feelings for her, but still...

"So are they saying it's foul play?"

"Not exactly. Could have still been an accident, but now they're looking into it more."

"Will you be interviewing people around—"

"Not me."

"Why not? Don't you do those sorts of things?"

"They got me on desk duty now. Long story."

"Wow, sorry," Sarah said. She couldn't get her mind off of what Patricia said, the cane, the bump on the head...

And, most importantly, the motive.

Maybe Emma was right...

She took a breath, let it out quickly, and spoke without thinking any further. "Adam, I heard that Patricia Greensmith was upset that her landlord—*you-know-who*—had raised her rent by twenty percent. She made a comment that was overheard by someone...basically, she said she'd clobber him over the head with her cane next chance she got."

"That's hearsay," Adam said, voice firm.

"But she has motive, she has the means, and even opportunity...I'm sure she was around the night of the...event."

Sarah had to catch herself from saying the M word.

"Again, no solid evidence."

"Should I file a report at the station?" Sarah asked.

"You could, but I doubt that would do much. And even if they did talk to her...well, let's just say most people aren't comfortable talking to the police about such matters, especially when such questions provoke the person to feel like they are being accused in any way."

"I could talk to her."

Adam was silent on the other end.

"Adam?"

"Don't worry about it."

"She knows me. I grew up here, and I'm not wearing a police uniform. I'll talk to her as a friend, see what I can find out."

"I don't think that's a good idea."

"I could talk to her, and then I'd let you know everything I found out. Maybe it could help in some way to bring justice to the deceased..."

Adam let out a huff. "Fine, but be discreet. And under no circumstances should you *accuse*—"

"Of course," Sarah said. "I have plenty of experience with delicate matters. You know my background."

"Right. Okay, well, I have to go. Endless paperwork is in my future…"

"Good luck."

"You too."

Adam ended the call, and Sarah put her phone back in her pocket.

She stared at the clock on her computer again, counting down the seconds until her grandpa and Emma finished their work. Once she let Emma know about the latest bit of information, she knew her cousin would say, "I told you so," but that didn't matter to her.

All that mattered was answering the questions that burned inside of her. Soon, she'd talk to Patricia Greensmith. Until then, all she could do was bide her time and come up with a plan of what to ask the sweet, little old lady who was now the first suspect in the suspicious incident of John Jacobs.

Maybe she had nothing to do with it, and an alibi would be quickly discovered.

Or maybe Emma was right, and Patricia Greensmith was a cunning old woman with a knack for putting up a masterful facade.

Only time would tell what Sarah would uncover.

CHAPTER 6

Time crawled by like an exhausted poodle, and Sarah thought Emma and her grandpa would never come out from the back office.

"What's taking them so long?" she wondered aloud, looking at the clock, urging the time to move quicker.

Sarah let out a sigh. Rugby and Misty walked out of the room together, and Sarah noted that those two seemed to be getting along much better. Next to her feet, Winston napped—the corgi hardly ever left her side.

A noise behind her and to the left caught her attention, and Sarah turned to see her cousin plodding out. Her eyes looked puffy and red, her hair disheveled.

"You look like you've been working in a coal mine," Sarah said.

Emma nodded. "I love Grandpa, I really do. But he can't seem to ever make up his mind. I'm literally pulling my hair out."

Sarah rose from the stool and stepped toward her cousin. "Emma, I heard something you might be interested in."

Emma looked at Sarah, expectantly. Sarah told her about what Adam Dunkin had said over the phone.

Emma's eyes lit up. "A bump on the back of the head?"

Sarah nodded.

"See, I told you...Looks can be deceiving." Emma put her hands on her hips and shook her head. "Her whole 'nice old lady' schtick is a facade."

"Maybe. We still don't know for sure."

"It's too bad," Emma continued. "I really like her tea."

Sarah was about to repeat herself about them not knowing for sure it was Patricia but thought better of it. Sarah, herself, was becoming skeptical and a bit antsy to speak to her and find out. "Where's Grandpa?"

"Still back there poring over the order. It's finished, has been for an hour, but he insists on putting more elbow grease into it. He'll 'overcook it,' is what I think."

Sarah stepped over to her laptop and closed it, placing it in her backpack on the floor next to the stool.

"Where are you going?" Emma asked.

"I'm going to talk to Patricia."

"What? Really?"

"Yeah."

"But you're not the police…"

"Yesterday you were all gung-ho, and now—"

"I'm just saying, you're not the cops. Where's Adam?"

"Tied up. I talked to him, it's cool. I'm not going to ask anything that'll sound like I'm accusing her of anything. I'm just a citizen talking to another citizen. It'll be innocent-sounding, so I might even have a better chance of getting some info to feed to the authorities."

"I'm going with."

"No, you stay here. We both know Grandpa is probably going to be back there awhile yet, and someone needs to watch the storefront."

"Aren't you going to take Rugby?"

"No. Patricia isn't a big fan of dogs, especially in her fancy establishment."

Emma nodded and took Sarah's place behind the counter without another word.

"Be right back," Sarah said, and hurried out of the shop before her cousin could protest her decision.

Sarah made her way to Patricia's Tea Room, and once inside, saw the same young man behind the counter. Off to her left, a petite woman sat, occupying one of the tables. She sipped tea and stared out the window onto the street.

"Mrs. Greensmith?"

The woman turned to look at Sarah, a puzzled look on her face. Then, as if a light switch had been flipped, her face lit up in recognition.

"Sarah? Is that really you?"

Sarah nodded. "How are you, Mrs. Greensmith?"

The woman tried to correct her posture, wincing in pain. "I've seen better days. Been a bit under the weather lately. Speaking of, nasty storm last night, eh?"

"Yeah, it was wicked. Are you feeling okay?"

"I'm fine," she said. "I'm a lucky old woman to have both of my grandkids to help out around the shop." She motioned toward the man behind the counter, who nodded at them, aware he was being talked about.

Before Sarah could reply, a young woman—perhaps about Sarah's age—came into the shop from the rear boardwalk entrance.

"Danny," the woman said, "take your break."

Danny gave a relieved look, and poured himself a cup of tea. He stepped out the back of the shop, probably eager to relax outside in the late-morning sun.

The young woman saw Sarah and came over, waving.

Patricia Greensmith said, "Sarah, you remember my granddaughter, Nancy?"

"Of course. How are you, Nancy?" Sarah asked.

"I'm good. Just hustling to get things ready for the season," Nancy said with a smile.

"Oh, Nancy is such a peach, always helping me out," Patricia said. "And Danny, too, of course."

At the mention of Danny, Sarah caught Nancy flashing a momentary sour face, quickly correcting herself before her nana noticed.

"The boy has really turned a new leaf," Patricia continued, without skipping a beat. "He came for a visit for a few weeks, and just in time, when Nancy and I really need the extra help."

"Nana, you know I would've been able to take care of everything just fine. I always do."

"I know, dear," Patricia said, taking Nancy's hand and patting it, "but you need breaks too…and a life. I feel I'm keeping you from finding a nice boy and settling down."

Nancy's cheeks flushed pink from her Nana's statement, but her eyes were kind. "No, Nana. Don't ever think that. I love helping you."

Patricia smiled.

Nancy looked at Sarah. "Nana thinks she's a burden."

Sarah chuckled.

Just then, a customer came through the door, bells jingling. "Well, sorry to cut this short," Nancy said, "but I'm being summoned. Would you like me to bring you anything?"

"No, I'm good. Thanks," Sarah said.

"Don't be silly," Patricia said, waving her hand at Sarah. "At least have some tea. On the house."

"Oh no, I couldn't."

"I haven't seen you in a while, what? How long has it been?"

"At least two years," Sarah said.

"I'll bring you our tea of the day," Nancy said. "Let me just take care of this customer and I'll bring it to you." Nancy turned to her Nana. "Nana, you want your chamomile green tea?"

Patricia nodded. "Thank you, dear."

Nancy trotted off. Sarah could hear her greeting the customer in the distance. "So, Nancy really helps you out around here."

"Why, yes. Always has. Since she was a teenager in high school, she would work part-time, after her studies, of course, and full-time in the summer."

"That's so sweet of her."

"Yes, and Danny has been equally sweet. He's been doing all the heavy lifting around here lately and I'm so proud of him. He held my hand in the hospital." Patricia paused, looking around, and leaned forward. "Don't tell him I told you this, but I think I heard him crying and praying for me. Poor guy was devastated."

"What happened that you were in the hospital?"

"My ticker's not what it used to be," she said, pressing one hand against her chest. "Nancy found me on the floor, right over there." Patricia pointed to the floor by the counter. "Nancy was hysterical. It was Danny who took me to the hospital."

"I'm sorry."

"You shouldn't be sorry, dear. You're not the one who gave me a bad heart," Patricia said, with a laugh.

The front door opened as more customers filed in. Nancy walked over briskly with two sets of porcelain tea cups and saucers on a serving tray lined with paper doilies. She set down the serving tray and placed one small cup in front of Sarah and the other in front of Patricia. "There you go. Enjoy," she said and hurried off to serve the next customer.

"Did they say what might have been the cause?" Sarah asked.

"The doctor's said it could have been due to stress. Most women my age are retired, but I'm still kicking. Busy as a bee. Though, my grandkids think it was the stress of the rent increase coupled with getting ready for the season."

"Yes, I heard that John Jacobs increased everyone's rent."

"By twenty percent," Patricia said, her eyes wide, and Sarah could see a tinge of anger behind them.

"You do know he's—"

"Dead. Yeah, I know about that."

Sarah took a breath, then said what was on her mind without another moment's hesitation. "I heard you threatened him."

Patricia froze. "Threatened? I don't threaten anyone. It's not the way I was raised."

"I heard you said you were going to clobber him over the head with your cane."

Sarah studied Patricia's face as she asked the question. It seemed like a light went on in Patricia's eyes suddenly. "Oh, that! Well, I didn't mean that. He just roused me up that day. He had come in here to cause trouble."

"About the rent increase?" Sarah said.

"No, he told everyone about the rent increase well over a week ago."

"Oh, what day did you threaten him, then?"

"The day before he died, I think."

Sarah's eyes went wide. "What? What happened?"

"He comes in here and asks me about my oatmeal cookies, needs a box of them for a dinner party or something like that. I tell him that I can whip up a fresh batch in 24 hours. I got other orders, you know. That's not good enough for him. He needs them tonight!" Patricia paused, taking a sip of her tea. "I don't normally do this, but I think, what the heck, I understand that we all get into a bind from time to time, and I offer to get them done before this party, but he'll have to pay extra for a rush order and to come back in five hours. He agrees. He comes back and he wants to try one of the cookies. I have to admit, I was taken back by this, as everyone knows my oatmeal cookies."

"Does he normally order oatmeal cookies?"

"Come to think of it, no. I don't think he's ever ordered an oatmeal cookie here," Patricia said, thinking. "Or any cookie, for that matter."

"Hm." Maybe he's just not into cookies, Sarah thought. "So, what happened next?"

"Well, he comes back, tries the cookie, and spits it out in front of me and several of my customers. He says that they are no good. I ask him why, what's wrong with them? And he says that they are too dry and way too sweet."

"Oh, boy."

"'Oh, boy' is right," Patricia said. "Of course, I was offended, and he embarrassed me in front of my customers. I apologized to him and told him I could make him something else. I mean, I'm not going to adjust an old family recipe just to his liking. He tells me to forget about it. He doesn't have the time, and goes to walk away. I told him to hold up. He still owes me for the cookies, including the rush-order fee. That was the deal. He says no way is he going to pay for something as disgusting as those cookies."

Sarah gasped. "He said that in front of your customers?"

"Word for word. Practically yelled it to the heavens. I'll never forget," Patricia said, shaking her head. "Well," Patricia paused, face flushed. "That's when, I guess you can say, I threatened him. Told him that I would clobber him over the head the next chance I got. He laughs and walks out the door without paying a single cent. By then, the show was over, and the remaining customers left. Can you believe that? Next thing I know, my chest begins to tighten and I'm on the floor, and the next morning, I wake up in the hospital and I hear John Jacobs has drowned."

Patricia hesitated, then continued, "I'm ashamed to say this but, I remember my first thought was 'good for him.' But I immediately felt guilty for even thinking like that. He wasn't a well-liked man, but no one deserves to drown."

Sarah nodded, also feeling ashamed of herself to think it would be Patricia who was behind John Jacobs' death. In fact, how could she think that this poor woman would even have the ability or strength to pull off a crime like that? Sarah could kick herself for allowing her cousin to get into her head. "I'm so sorry for everything you went through."

Sarah hurried home. She had to get to her cousin and let her know that Patricia had more than a solid alibi the night of John Jacobs' death. Not only did she have witnesses of her whereabouts that night, but she had been tended to by nurses and doctors all night.

Inside the store, Rugby and Winston played, and Emma shook her head. "These dogs are driving me crazy."

Larry came out from the back office, his hair disheveled.

"How's the order going?" Sarah asked.

Larry shook his head, like a doctor delivering bad news through somber body language. "I need a break. I think I'll take over watching the store awhile." Larry sat down behind the counter.

"I think that's a good idea," Sarah said. She turned to her cousin. "Hey, Emma, what do you say we take these dogs for a walk? What do you think?" Sarah gave her cousin a wink, the signal that she had a secret to tell.

At the word "walk," Rugby sprung up, hopping around in circles.

"Please! Let's," Emma said.

They leashed up the dogs and she and Emma said goodbye to their grandpa and stepped out onto the street. Winston walked alongside Sarah, leash slacked, unlike Rugby, who pulled a bit for the first five minutes of the walk, with excitement. Sarah was surprised at how well Winston walked. Whoever his owner was, they had definitely spent time training him.

They walked past the Tea Room, and Emma turned to Sarah. "So, what's going on? Did you talk to Patricia?"

"Yeah, but—" Sarah started. Out of the corner of her eye, she saw a figure standing between the Tea Room and the neighboring building.

"Oh, geez," Emma said to the man, who Sarah recognized as Patricia Greensmith's grandson, Danny. "You scared me half to death."

"Sorry," Danny said. He looked at the dogs, a puzzled look on his face. "New dog?"

"We found him," Sarah said. "Spread the word that we found a corgi named Winston last night, right before the storm hit."

Danny didn't say a word, still focused on the dogs.

Before he could say what was on his mind, Sarah and Emma both waved and strode off.

"What a goof," Emma said. "So, tell me about what you learned from his nana. Is she the murderer?"

"First, they still don't know if there was any foul play —still classified as an accident. Grandpa was right, you do jump to con—"

"So do you," Emma cut in. "Otherwise you wouldn't have gone to talk to our only *suspect*."

"Well, one thing I know for sure is that it wasn't her."

"How do you know for sure?"

"Because she has a solid alibi with many witnesses on her that entire night, including paperwork that will corroborate her whereabouts."

Emma looked at Sarah, confused. "Where was she?"

"Cascade Memorial Hospital. She had problems with her heart that day and she collapsed. Danny rushed her to the hospital."

Emma's mouth dropped. "How come I didn't hear about this?"

"You know Patricia, she doesn't give everything away unless you ask."

"What about the threat?"

Sarah explained Patricia's story about the oatmeal cookies and John Jacobs.

"Wow. Poor Patricia. First, her cookies are insulted, and then she has a heart attack."

"And then we suspect her of foul play," Sarah added.

As they walked along, Sarah felt the sun warm her face. She hadn't worn sunscreen, and she made a note to remember for next time—the last thing she wanted was another lobster face this summer.

Both Rugby and Winston were sluggish by the time they made it to the end of the strip and back. There were more people than when Sarah had arrived, the only indication that the busy season was soon to arrive. Shop owners were cleaning their display windows. Off-season vacationers were enjoying one last bit of calm before the true storm that would sweep across the Cove. Its pristine beaches, beautiful sunsets, and historic lighthouse were a magnet for off-season vacationers and summer tourists alike, the latter enjoying the shops, wake boarding, parasailing, and the small amusement park at the end of the boardwalk that would soon be lit up and alive again.

They stopped into the ice cream shop and ordered two vanilla and chocolate swirl cones. They took their treats out and sat on a bench, looking out at the businesses on the opposite side.

"I'm glad it's just a coincidence and still an accident," Sarah said.

Emma nodded, but said nothing.

Sarah continued, "I can't imagine what a murderer would do to our little town this summer."

"Do you think tourists would catch wind of that and not come?"

"Probably."

Sarah sat with her cousin and thought about what would happen to their town, the local businesses, her grandpa...

"I bet it's all just in our heads," Sarah said, finishing her ice cream cone. She hoped that was true.

If not, the next two weeks would be very interesting if a killer were on the loose.

CHAPTER 7

Once finished with their ice cream cones, Sarah and Emma walked the dogs across the street, and strode along the sand-swept walkway until they reached their grandpa's boutique. An intermittent breeze cooled Sarah's skin, giving her much needed reprieve from the heat.

"Cover for me, Emma," Larry said the moment they were in the main shop area. "I'm going to make some lunch."

"It's about time," Emma said, taking Larry's place.

"Come with me," Larry said to Sarah. He followed her, both dogs now with them, and they made their way up to the apartment. Once there, she closed the door and saw her grandpa lumber toward the kitchen.

Sarah let the dogs off their leashes, and they bolted

across the kitchen to their bowls of food and water. Misty had just finished her food and leapt up onto a chair, out of the way of the two wild dogs, licking her paw to clean her face.

Sarah heard them crunching on kibble as she kicked off her shoes and made her way to the kitchen table.

"What's this?" Sarah asked, though she didn't have to. It was one of Grandma's scrapbooks. "Is Grandma back already?"

"Oh heavens, no," Larry said, fishing ingredients out of the fridge. "I just like paging through them. Memory lane and all…"

Sarah sat down and leafed through the scrapbook. "Wow, these pictures are ancient."

"Your grandma and I always said that her scrapbooks belonged in the library—good source of local lore."

"A visual history book."

Larry walked over to her and stood beside her chair, craning his neck to see what page she was on.

"Exactly. Sometimes she writes captions," Larry said, and pointed to handwritten notes below one of the pictures.

"I can't read that," Sarah said, squinting.

"Hmm, let's see," Larry said, leaning closer. "Walter Greensmith and George Jacobs."

Sarah recognized both last names.

"Greensmith, is that…"

"Patricia's late husband, yes," Larry said, index finger tapping against the man on the left.

"And this man on the right…"

"That's John Jacobs' father. He's gone too."

"Did you know them?"

"Of course, I've been here long enough to know about their firm."

"Firm?"

"Let's just say, they were longtime partners. Owned a lot of the land in the area, back when this town was even smaller than it is now, and we had nothing more than a dirt road, the lighthouse, and the pier. Well, a little more than that, but you get the picture."

Sarah thought about this new information, though it was no surprise that Patricia Greensmith had more than one connection to John Jacobs. It was a town where everyone knew everyone else, and gossip flew around faster than the seagulls.

"Hmm," Sarah said, and paged through the scrapbook.

"Lots of goodies in there," Larry said. "See, there's me and your grandma before we even moved down here. Well before you were a twinkle in your father's eyes."

Sarah looked at the old picture. Larry's hair was still just as curly and light-colored, though it was hard to tell what shade of blond it was in the black and white photo. She gazed upon her grandmother, who was probably Sarah's current age in the picture.

"Those were the good old days," Larry said, staring intently at the picture. "Hopefully you'll get to see that amazing woman before you go."

"I hope so too."

"You can keep paging through," Larry said. "I need to cook up some grub."

Larry walked toward his array of ingredients and started up the stove's burners to make bacon for BLTs.

Sarah continued to page through the scrapbook, seeing a bunch of familiar faces and some not-so-familiar faces. Eventually, she closed the book when she smelled the completed lunch.

"Here you go," Larry said, putting a plate off to the side of the book. Larry picked up the book and carried it into the living room. There, she saw him place it on a bookshelf. She'd have to revisit that scrapbook again, if not just to take another peek into the past.

Finishing her lunch, Sarah felt the necklace around her neck, the antique pendant's weight noticeable. She took off the locket and set it down on the table, then took her plate into the kitchen, putting it in the dishwasher.

Sarah got her sneakers on and started toward the

door to head back down to the boutique. She heard Larry's voice behind her. "I'm going to clean up," he said. "I'll be down in a jiffy."

Down in the boutique, Sarah saw Emma practically falling asleep behind the counter. Rugby and Winston raced over to where Emma sat, startling her. She and Misty were much alike, and when resting, preferred to be left alone. Now, with a bustle of activity, Emma simply rose from the stool and stretched toward the ceiling.

Larry came in a moment later, and Sarah turned to see him sauntering in, surprised that he cleaned up so quickly. He looked like he was a man on a mission. Stepping behind the counter, he pressed a few buttons on the register. The register drawer flew open and he stared down at the different denominations of bills and coins.

"Did we make any sales today?" Larry asked, placing a Tupperware container with Emma's BLT in it on the counter next to the register.

Emma shifted her weight to one side, eyeing up her lunch. "A woman came in with her dachshund and bought a few items. Twenty dollars, maybe."

"That's a start," Larry said, nodding.

"Yeah," Emma said, pulling off the top of the Tupperware and revealing her sandwich. "We'll have a lot more than that in sales by lunch time when the busy season hits."

Larry closed the register drawer and let out a sigh. "Let's hope so."

"We did well last year."

"I know, but it's been getting tougher and tougher."

Sarah made her way over to the counter and looked under it. She'd placed the flyers she made for Winston in one of the drawers, and found them quickly. "I'm going to walk around and spread word about Winston."

"Good idea," Larry said. "Don't forget to tack a few of those flyers to the telephone poles."

"I will. I'm taking the dogs with me."

Sarah got the dogs leashed up and was out the door only a few minutes later.

Their walk was longer than usual that afternoon. Sarah made one stop after another, going into whatever businesses were open. Half of them still weren't, so she made note that she'd have to cycle back through the town in the coming days as more and more of the family businesses got ready.

She tacked a few flyers to a pole here and a bulletin board there. In the small, corner grocery store, she utilized a large open space on the community cork board. She was glad that she went with neon-green paper, as the flyer really stood out among all the black and white announcements, business cards, and flyers.

Sarah said hello to many people she'd seen every summer. She stopped in to see Gordy, the owner of the delicatessen, where she got a few complimentary slices of salami and bologna. The next stop was Surf's Up, an off-the-wall surf shop run by a mother and her twin daughters, Faye and Isabella. In that shop, Rugby and Winston both enjoyed being petted by the twins, their mother, and several of the customers who were browsing around.

So far, nobody had any clue as to who Winston belonged to.

"Come on, guys," Sarah said to her two canine companions and pressed on to continue their journey across town.

Next stop was the Banana Hammock Bar and Grill. The hostess, Kacey, was a childhood friend of Sarah and Emma. She talked briefly with her, and introduced her to the dogs, highlighting the fact that she'd just found Winston. Kacey, unfortunately, hadn't heard of anyone looking for their lost dog, but agreed to take a flyer and post it near the entrance.

A few more stops later, Sarah found herself at the

end of the strip, a barren area of dunes and patches of beachgrass beyond that flanked the road leading to the next town, a few miles away.

"The end of the line," Sarah said, and lead the way back toward the middle of town, where her grandpa's boutique was.

It took about twenty minutes for her to make it back to the boutique, their pace relaxed. She chalked it up to the fact that both dogs were exhausted, but she felt her legs ache. In the city, she'd usually taken public transport, which was within a short walk from her apartment. Here, it was typically easier to walk around, especially since her grandpa's place was at the midway point.

Back inside the boutique, Sarah smiled when she saw her grandpa.

"Why are you wearing that thing?" she asked.

Larry feigned innocence, tapping the old, antique pendant lightly, letting it swing back and forth across his chest. "Don't you think it fits my Hawaiian shirt?"

Sarah let the dogs off the leash, and they rushed to the nearby water bowls. She heard them lapping up water eagerly.

"It suits you well," she said.

Larry took the necklace off and hung it up on a hook

behind the counter. Apparently, he thought the pendant clashed with his attire.

"Where's Emma?" Sarah asked.

"Upstairs taking a nap. Guess I'm driving her nuts again—she just doesn't get my humor, is all." Larry waggled his eyebrows, two miniature gray caterpillars resting above his eyes.

"Neither do I," Sarah said, winking at him.

"I should go up and get dinner ready."

"No chocolate cake for dinner tonight?"

"Well," Larry said, hand on chin, rubbing his gray stubble, "we do have half of it left..."

"Kidding, Grandpa."

"Could you watch the store for a while?"

"Sure. I'll be up later if I'm hungry."

"I'll text you and let you know when it's ready."

Larry picked up Misty and took her along with him as he made his way up to the apartment.

In the back office, Sarah heard Rugby and Winston snoring softly.

Looking at her computer, she saw the store would be closing in fifteen minutes. She busied herself by ensuring all the displays looked presentable. She cleaned the glass displays, proud to see them glean as a result of her efforts. Then, she went back into the office, trying hard not to disturb the dogs.

The front door's bell jingled again.

"Be right out," she called, then hurried out.

A man in black rushed out of the door, as if he were startled by her presence. The door swung back shut, the jingle of the bells getting lost in the growing silence.

"I guess he went in the wrong door," she muttered, figuring it was the same man in black she saw when the storm started up the other day.

Checking the time again, she saw it was a few minutes past closing time.

"Might as well enjoy this calm before it gets busier next week," she said.

She padded over to the entrance and turned the lock. A few paces to the left, she pulled the chain on the OPEN sign so its red and blue lights would cease their flashing.

She lowered some of the lights and went back into her grandpa's office, settling down at his desk with her laptop. Instead of going upstairs, she decided she'd like some alone time to go through her emails and browse the internet for knitting patterns and the like.

Hours passed, and her eyes grew heavy. She reached into her pocket to check her phone, thinking it weird that her grandpa hadn't texted her yet.

"Oh jeez," she said, noticing she forgot to take her phone off silent mode again.

She eyed the texts and read the first text aloud:

"Dinner is server! Love, Grandpa."

Then, "Server = Severed."

Sarah giggled. He always had issues using his "new-fangled telephonic apparatus," as he so eloquently called it.

She read the final text: "Ugh. Not 'Severed'...that's a bit morbid. If you couldn't tell, I meant to say 'Served.' If you don't come up soon, I'll wrap it up for you to eat later. Love, Grandpa."

Sarah smiled, and took her phone off its silent mode before texting her grandpa back.

"Thanks, Grandpa," she said aloud, letting her smartphone's voice recognition feature do its magic. "I'll be up in a little bit. Just finishing up on some stuff."

Once she reread the text to ensure no Grandpa-style typos were there, she sent the message and pocketed the phone.

She stepped over to the seventies-style couch that sat off on the other side of the office and laid down. Winston jumped up and snuggled next to her for warmth while Rugby still snored on the floor.

"Hey, boy. Come to join me?" He licked her hand and made himself more comfortable. She was happy to have Winston and worried what would happen when his rightful owners were found. He had become so attached to her. Or was it that she had become so attached to him?

She closed her eyes for a moment, then a short time later—or perhaps an hour or two later—she heard a loud bang that made her and Winston jump.

CHAPTER 8

Sarah sat bolt upright, hearing both dogs hollering at the subsequent sound.

"What in the world..." Sarah said, swinging herself off of the couch, stepping hesitantly toward the door that lead to the boutique's showroom, and to whatever —or whoever—was making that noise. Sarah peeked around the corner into the boutique and then heard the noise again. Something at the front door, like someone was trying to pry it open.

By the aid of the moonlight, she spotted a figure in the window of the front door. Sarah's vision narrowed as she tried her best to focus on who it was. No facial features were visible, since whoever was out there was wearing a hood. The person was a silhouette against the moonlight.

Rugby scrambled toward the door, carrying on, a snarl in his bark.

It was unlike Rugby to snarl, or bare his teeth, but he was likely reacting to her own body's response to what was happening: clenching fists, clammy skin, and the unmistakable sensation of an adrenaline rush.

All of this happened in a matter of seconds.

Sarah no more than blinked before the silhouette at the door disappeared like a phantom.

Not more than thirty seconds later, Larry emerged from the door that lead up to the apartment. He flicked the lights on, a look of panic on his face. "Are you okay? I heard all sorts of commotion going on down here."

"Did you see him?"

"Who?"

Sarah told her grandpa about the man who, not more than a minute before, was trying to break through the front door to the shop.

"No, didn't see anyone."

Sarah furrowed her brows and stared at the door.

Questions swirled in her mind.

Who was out there? Why were they trying to break in? And when did break-ins become a thing in Cascade Cove?

Sarah was determined to get to the bottom of this. Reaching in her pocket, she grabbed her phone.

"What are you doing?" Larry asked.

"Calling Adam Dunkin."

Sarah watched as Adam Dunkin examined the door with a flashlight, then turned to look at Larry, who paced back and forth in the front of his boutique between the displays of dog scarves and catnip toys. Emma leaned up against the back wall of the boutique, yawning in her pajamas and cat slippers. All the lights in the store were on, a contrast to the darkness in the street and beyond. Sarah felt safe with the lights on, and especially safe now that Adam was there.

"Hmm," Adam said, running his fingers along the metal doorframe. "Looks like someone was trying to bust this open." Adam looked up at Larry. "Definitely forced entry. Well, attempted forced entry, I guess. Lucky for you, you got a pretty solid bolt on this door with a secure locking mechanism from the outside."

Larry stopped pacing. "I got the best door installed. At least, that's what they told me when I got it." Larry looked at Sarah and Emma. "Grandma was hounding me about getting a good door. So, I got her the best I could find."

Adam jotted a few notes onto a small pad of paper.

Emma straightened herself. "Well, if it's safe, I'm going back upstairs for some beauty rest. I'm beat."

"Good night, sweetie."

Emma had already started toward the door; her blonde, tousled bun on top of her head swayed tiredly as she shuffled her way back to bed. "Yeah, good night, everyone."

"So now what?" Larry asked, looking at Adam.

"I'll file this incident, and we'll keep our eyes and ears open."

Larry nodded, still pacing and running his hands through his hair.

"You don't have any security cameras outside, do you?" Adam asked. "Or any in here aiming toward the door?"

Larry stopped pacing and laughed, a reaction that surprised Sarah.

"This town is as safe as a foam pit, Mr. Dunkin."

"So, no cameras, then?"

Larry shook his head. "No, never even crossed my mind, to be honest."

"I see."

"I don't even lock my apartment door—never so much as a single napkin has been out of place."

"Right, but the store..."

"Of course, I lock up the store, obviously." Larry

motioned with one hand toward the scraped doorframe. "But most of the time, I think even locking up the store is pointless...unless it's the busy season."

"I see," Adam said, writing more notes, then pocketing his pad and pen.

Just then, the door opened, and Sarah jumped. It was just the other police officer that had come with Adam. "I double-checked the perimeter," the man said. "I didn't find anything."

"Thanks, Finley. I'll meet you in the car."

"Sure thing, Dunkin, I'll get started on the paperwork."

"Thank you. I'll be out in a minute; I'm almost done."

Finley walked out to the patrol car.

Adam turned to Larry. "Mr. Shores, this is unrelated, but since I'm here, I have to ask."

"Yeah?"

"I'm looking for someone. A man by the name of..." Adam fished into his pocket and pulled out the pad again, flipping through the pages. "I'm looking for Orloff Minsky." Adam began reading off a description from his pad, "He's Russian, tall, with dark hair, green eyes, and a raven tattooed on the right side of his neck." He looked up at Larry. "He's a neighbor of yours. Have you seen him lately?"

Larry thought for a moment, then said, "Can't say that I

have. Barely know the guy. He's fairly new around here and I haven't had a chance to meet him properly yet. Why?"

"We're just looking for him."

"Oh, I'm sorry, Adam. But I haven't seen him recently."

"Could you let me know if you do?"

"Of course."

Sarah walked over and stopped next to Larry. "Grandpa, why don't you go to bed and I'll take it from here. You have to finish up your orders tomorrow."

"That's right. That order." Larry turned to Adam. "Getting ready for the season. You know how that gets."

Adam smiled. "Yes, Mr. Shores. I know."

"Well, if you don't need me for anything else…"

"No, sir."

"Then I'll bid you both good night." Larry reached over and shook Adam's hand and then gave Sarah a hug. "Don't stay up too late," he whispered to Sarah, wiggling his caterpillar brows. Sarah swatted Larry and he turned to walk away. Before he closed the door behind him, he said, "Sarah, don't forget to make sure everything is secure. I still can't believe this happened." He mumbled a few more things while closing the door.

Sarah turned to Adam. "Does this have anything to do with the Jacobs case?"

Adam's face grew grim. He gazed back at Sarah. "Listen, I'll tell you since he's your neighbor, and I'm looking out for you and your family. But you have to promise to keep this between us. I could get in trouble if—"

"You can count on me," she said.

"Good."

"So, what's going on?"

"Well, some of our people at the station did a bit more digging, especially since the bump was discovered on the back of the victim's head. Most people we interviewed have rock-solid alibis." Giving Sarah a look, Adam continued, "Including Mrs. Patricia Greensmith—we followed up with the hospital, and it all checks out that she was there during the incident."

Sarah nodded. She was glad Patricia had been quickly exonerated.

Adam looked back down at his legal pad. "But we have yet to question Mr. Minsky."

"How does he connect to Jacobs?"

"He was his gardener, knew the lay of the land around the Jacobs estate. Interesting thing we found was that Mr. Jacobs fired him the day of his death—at the end of his shift at five o'clock."

Sarah put her finger to her chin. "So, Jacobs fires his

gardener, Orloff, and then the next day, the old man's body is found by the fishermen."

"That about sums it up."

"Do you have a weapon?" Sarah asked. She figured whatever blunt object Orloff might've used to hit his former boss over the head before dumping his body would have to be somewhere. Perhaps it was one of his gardening tools…Whatever the weapon, she realized whoever killed Mr. Jacobs wouldn't have been so careless as to leave the murder weapon lying around for anyone to find. Still, she had to ask.

Adam shook his head. "No weapon found."

"Anything else?" she asked.

"No," Adam said. "And, to be clear, we simply need to find Orloff to ask him a few questions. He's relatively new in town, and due to the suspicious nature of having been fired the day before Mr. Jacobs' body was found, it would suggest a clear motive. Once we question him, we'll be able to determine if he has a solid alibi or not."

Sarah nodded. "Of course. Innocent until proven guilty."

Adam wrote down a few more notes in his pad, then slid it into his pocket. "That's the name of the game. But as I said, we're just dotting every 'I' and crossing every 'T.' There's a chance that this is still just an accident, but we have to be sure we leave no stone unturned."

"Yeah, I get it," Sarah said. "Hey, do you think it's possible this Orloff guy tried to break into the shop?"

"Doubtful," Adam said. "Murder and burglary are two different species. And if you ask me, Orloff is looking more like the murdering type. Burglary is more common than your grandfather thinks. His store just hasn't been targeted before."

Sarah snickered. "Yeah, because, let's be honest, who would want to break into a pet boutique?"

Adam didn't share her humor. "Actually, these burglars don't care, as long as there's cash." Adam released tension from his face. "Listen, Sarah, don't underestimate anyone. Despite what people think around here at the Cove, we may not usually have a murder on our hands, but we do have drownings, accidents, and enough burglaries. Just be careful."

Sarah nodded. "I will."

"Well, I should be off."

"Thanks again for coming so quick."

"Of course," Adam said. "Besides, you calling me gave me a break from a stack of paperwork waiting for me at the station."

"Well, then, you're welcome."

"Thank you." He made his way to the door. "Make sure to lock up tight. And if you see Orloff or know where I can find him, call me on my cell." Adam looked at Sarah and flashed a smile.

"Sure thing," Sarah said, smiling back.

She watched as Adam Dunkin stepped out. He waited until she gave the thumbs up that the door was locked and secure. He tipped his hat and disappeared into the darkness. Her smile faded as the thought of a killer on the loose filled her mind.

Emma's the one who jumps to conclusions, she told herself. But Adam definitely hinted that he was leaning more toward murder. Murder at Cascade Cove. A panic at the pier. It didn't seem real.

But she couldn't help but jump to conclusions as well with the first solid pieces of the puzzle beginning to emerge.

CHAPTER 9

he next day, Sarah spent the morning at her grandpa's boutique, behind the counter, knitting a new dog sweater design she came up with last winter. She was trying to forget about what happened the night before. Rugby was laying in his usual spot by the stool behind the counter, with Winston nearby. Both were enjoying their late morning slumber.

Next to her, Emma was on her laptop, the keys clacking away.

"Okay," Emma said, "got the new website set up for Grandpa. Want to see it?"

Sarah put her knitting down and took Emma's laptop. "Wow, this is amazing."

"And check this out. If you click here, you can browse all our merch. And here," Emma moved the cursor to "cart" and clicked. "They can now purchase directly on the website."

"I can't believe you did this. Grandpa is going to love it."

"Yeah, so now it will be easier to make some money during the off-season online. We just have to build our brand more," Emma said, taking her laptop back.

Sarah was surprised, though Emma had always been a computer whiz. Something that didn't come quite as easily to Sarah.

"So, did Adam have anything else to say about the whole Jacobs murder when he was here last night?" Emma asked.

"Not a murder."

"Yet."

Sarah shook her head. "Actually, there is something."

"Really?" Emma's eyes went wide. "What?"

"Adam said he's looking for Orloff Minsky."

"Who?"

"You know Orloff. Grandpa says he lives in the apartment above the Bait and Tackle shop next door."

"Russian guy?"

"I think so."

"If he's the same guy I'm thinking of, he used to come into the shop by accident thinking it was the entrance to the stairway that led up to his apartment. So, what about Orloff did you find out? Did he kill John Jacobs?"

"Adam just needs to find him so he can be questioned."

"Until then, we have a killer on the loose…"

"Not exactly," Sarah said. "He's a suspect, not necessarily the murderer. Besides, they don't even know for sure that there's been any foul play. It's just that Orloff was fired the day of the incident."

Emma rose up from her stool. "No way! Don't you see—"

"Yeah, it's a big coincidence. I know."

"Gigantic coincidence. I mean, c'mon, Sarah. That's one big, stinking motive."

"Among others," Sarah corrected. "Don't forget Jacobs raising the rent. That's a big enough motive for a lot of people in this town. And do you remember Patricia Greensmith's threat and the bump on the head? That was an awfully big coincidence, and that fell through."

"Touché. But Orloff is fairly new in town. First job he was fired at, so we don't know what his temperament is."

"And we don't have a baseline for it, either," Sarah added.

Emma's phone chimed, and she stepped out from behind the counter.

"Where are you going?" Sarah asked.

"Grandpa is out beyond the Cove and ran out of gas again."

"Again?"

"Yeah, it's a once-a-month thing. Another fun quirk to add to his list."

"Why doesn't he, you know, remember to fill up his gas tank?"

"It's his fuel gauge. It's broken. Always shows empty, but somehow he figures, since it's broken, it's always wrong. Except when it's not…"

"Like now."

Emma rolled her eyes.

"Why doesn't he get his fuel gauge fixed?" Sarah asked.

"The question should be, 'Why is he still driving a Pinto from the early '70s?'"

"It's Grandpa we're talking about here," Sarah said, grinning. "You really had to ask?"

"Bah," Emma said, rushing off to save the day for their grandpa. Before leaving, she called over her shoulder, "Keep your eyes peeled, Sarah! The Cascade Cove Killer is on the loose!"

It was Sarah's turn to roll her eyes.

She heard the corgi whine by her side.

"It's okay, Winston," she said, leaning down to pet the dog. "I'll protect you."

Rugby huffed, and Sarah used her free hand to rub his back.

"You guys want a Fudderdog Treat?"

Both dogs' ears perked up, and she grabbed two treats, handing one to each. They strode off in separate directions. The boutique was quiet, with the exception of their crunching and Misty's purring somewhere in the back office.

The bell on the door leading to the boardwalk rang, and she saw a woman in a beautiful summer dress walking in. She wore a brimmed hat, and Sarah immediately recognized her.

"Hi, Marigold."

"Good morning, Sarah. How are you today?"

"Living the dream. How about you?"

Marigold looked around the store, then she looked back at Sarah. "Good. Just enjoying the warm weather. Decided to take a nice stroll on the boardwalk, and I finally had the chance to go riding this morning."

"Riding?"

"Yes, I have stables at my vineyard now."

"Oh, that must be nice," Sarah said with a smile.

"It's heavenly." Marigold put her gloved hand to her

chest. "I love my horses," Marigold said, stepping around the shop, browsing.

"Anything I can help you find?"

"Actually, I came in to get my friend something for her dog, Ruffles."

"Cute name."

"It's a Yorkshire terrier. Or what I call a Yorkshire *terror*."

Sarah chuckled and came out from behind the counter. "They each have their own personalities."

"So true," Marigold said, picking up a squeaky toy. She pressed it, then let it go. It gave a loud *squeak*.

Rugby and Winston both bolted out from their respective sides of the boutique.

"Oh, well, what do we have here?" Marigold said, looking down at the dogs. "They are adorable. Both yours?"

"The yellow lab is. His name's Rugby."

"And this smaller fellow?"

"He followed me home before the storm the other night. I put flyers up around town."

"Oh, yes, how could I miss those signs. That's a shame that he's lost, but at least he found a nice person to watch after him until he finds his rightful owners."

Sarah smiled, appreciative of the compliment. She didn't understand what Emma's beef was with

Marigold. She seemed so sweet, and Sarah considered herself to be a pretty good judge of character.

Marigold leaned down to pet each dog on the head, then glanced at the elegant gold watch on her wrist. "My goodness, I lost track of the time." She grabbed a few items and placed them on the counter.

Sarah rung her up and said, "It's so nice to see you again."

"The pleasure is all mine," Marigold said, putting her sunglasses on.

Placing her items in a large paper bag with "Larry's Pawfect Boutique" printed on it, Sarah handed them to Marigold.

"Good day, Sarah," Marigold said, then strode out with the bag swinging by her side.

The doorbell chimed on her way back out to the boardwalk.

Sarah was left with the silence of the empty boutique.

An hour later, Emma returned to the boutique after "rescuing" Grandpa. Sarah leashed up the dogs and set out to spend the rest of the afternoon roaming around

Cascade Cove. The weather was perfect, and she remembered to apply her sunscreen this time.

Rugby and Winston galloped along, eager to explore with Sarah.

Though she was concerned about the possibility of there being a killer on the loose, Sarah figured it could just as well still be an accident.

She pushed all thoughts of murder and deception to the back of her mind.

Today was hers to enjoy.

She was on vacation, after all.

"Want to go to Henry Fudderman's?" she asked her companions.

Both responded by bounding forward lightly, pulling her toward the bakery as if they knew that's where the famed Henry Fudderman was.

"I'll take that as a yes," she said, trying to keep up with the excited duo.

She approached the bakery, and on her way in, she saw a couple coming out.

Both wore smiles on their faces.

That was a clear sign that someone had just enjoyed one of Fudderman's many amazing creations.

Inside the bakery, Henry waved hello. His face was jolly red, as usual, matching the bowtie tucked under his chin, smile beaming.

"Sarah! Did your grandfather enjoy his Boardwalk Fudge Cake?"

"More than you could know."

"Hopefully it didn't ruin his dinner."

Sarah felt the leashes tug slightly. "It *was* his dinner!"

Henry guffawed. "Sounds like Larry."

"Pretty much."

The old baker leaned over the counter, eyeing the corgi curiously. "Is that the fellow you mentioned? The one on your flyer?"

Sarah turned and saw her flyer on a board near the bakery's entrance. "Yeah."

"He's quite the charmer. Nobody came forward as his owner?"

"Not yet."

"I'll keep spreading the word," Henry said.

"Thanks."

Sarah ordered a Cascade Cruller, and Henry placed one on a plate. "Just made these this morning."

She paid and accepted the plate, taking it over to a table.

Taking a bite, she sighed. Her mouth watered instantly as the sweet, sugary pastry filled her mouth. It was crisp on the outside, and soft and fluffy on the inside. "Incredible."

Henry interrupted her blissful moment. "So, did you hear?" he asked.

"Hear what?"

"Word is, in addition to the bump on the old man's head, they found signs of a struggle."

Sarah's eyes widened. "What clues told them that?"

"Couldn't tell ya. I'm not into all the forensic lingo and jargon. But from what I've heard, they're ruling it out being an accident."

"Really?"

"Yeah. Someone must've had it in for Jacobs, and they took care of him."

Sarah's mind went directly to Mr. Jacobs' gardener, Orloff. She didn't know what he looked like, nor had she met the guy yet. But from what she had gathered so far, he definitely would have it in for Jacobs. She had to remind herself that this was still hearsay. She could practically hear Adam's voice echo in her mind. The rumor mill in Cascade Cove was churning at full force, like a riptide ready to sweep away anyone unable—or unwilling—to work through the problem objectively.

"Is that so?" Sarah said, nibbling on her cruller.

"Afraid it is. And right before the busy season. If it's confirmed and goes to print…"

"It'll be okay."

"The summer will be ruined. Nobody wants to vacation with a murderer on the loose."

Sarah nodded. The notion of there actually being a killer was apparently cemented in Henry's mind.

But it made sense.

If there were signs of a struggle, a bump on the head, and plenty of reasons for Jacobs to be out of the picture, then all signs pointed to it being more than an accident.

Finishing her cruller, she said, "I'm sure they'll catch whoever it is."

"I hope so."

On her way out, she waved bye to Henry. Before stepping out, she stopped dead in her tracks. She forgot to ask Henry something.

"Henry?"

"Yes, Sarah?"

"I have a question."

"I might have an answer."

"Have you seen Orloff Minsky?"

CHAPTER 10

*H*enry Fudderman's face scrunched up. Sarah knew he was considering her question. "Orloff Minsky?" he asked. "That Russian fellow?"

"Yeah. So, have you seen him around?"

Sarah waited for the man to reply.

She heard the faint sound of the dogs panting.

The refrigerated display case humming softly.

An old car puttered by on the main strip.

Finally, Henry broke the awkward silence. "Hmm, I can't say I have."

"When was the last time you saw him?"

"I haven't the faintest clue, to be honest. Why do you ask?"

"Just wondering." She kept her face neutral, trying not to give away the fact that Orloff might be a big piece of the Jacobs puzzle. A piece that was currently unaccounted for.

"If something comes to mind, I'll give Larry a call."

"Sounds good," Sarah said.

She and Henry Fudderman said their goodbyes. Back out on the main strip, Sarah strode back to her grandpa's.

The sun shone brightly in the cloudless sky, warming her face.

A light breeze tickled her skin, and she caught the unmistakable smell of salt water.

The dogs both walked on one side of her. A seagull swept overhead, squawking. Rugby seemed to notice the bird, but then set his gaze forward once again.

Up ahead, she saw her grandpa standing outside the boutique.

He turned and watched her and the dogs come toward him.

"Beautiful day," he said, shading his eyes with one hand.

"I heard you had some car trouble."

Larry shrugged.

"You know," Sarah continued, "they've been making cars since the seventies. You could pick up a newer model."

"Why fix what's not broken?"

"At least get the gas gauge fixed."

"I suppose I should," Larry said. "I just—"

"What?"

"I want to make sure your grandma can travel when she wants to. Plus, I love that old car. They don't make 'em like they used to."

Sarah smiled.

"You know, Grandpa, as a young girl, you were always my favorite. You're still my favorite."

Larry's face turned a light shade of red. "You sure know how to make an old man blush. Now, on to more serious matters…"

"Like what?"

"Well, I made another tray of brownies. You know, the one's with chocolate chips," he said, waggling his brows, "and they're begging to be gobbled down."

Sarah's smile grew wider. "You don't have to ask me twice."

Leave it to her grandpa to help remove any worry from her mind.

"Okay, you can go join Emma in the shop. I'll go up to get the brownies and bring them down."

"Sounds good."

Larry rushed up the steps toward his apartment, apparently eager for an afternoon treat.

Sarah took the dogs into the boutique.

Emma was stocking the shelves with what looked like a recent order.

"Wow, they ship fast," Sarah said, looking down at the box. "Do mom-and-pop boutique suppliers offer one-day delivery now?"

"I wish," Emma said, hanging gem-spotted collars of various colors and sizes on the wall. "This is an order we placed last week that just got here. But feel the inside of these collars." Emma held out one of the collars, a purple one, to Sarah. "They're so soft."

Sarah reached over to feel the inside. "Wow."

"And aren't they classy looking? They make them for both cats and dogs." Emma held up the tiny, purple collar, eyeing it up. "I think I'm going to give this one to Misty."

Misty, who was a ball of fur in her usual spot on the shelf, lifted her head to look at them. When she decided she wasn't interested, she yawned and tucked her head back into her own poof of fur.

Emma and Sarah exchanged glances and chuckled. "That Misty never looks amused," Sarah said.

"Not in the slightest."

The bell above the door rang, and Sarah saw a couple enter, a beagle at the end of a leash. They might've been the same couple who she saw leaving Fudderman's Bakery, but she couldn't be sure. She certainly didn't remember an accompanying beagle. On the cusp of busy-season, more and more people trickled into the area.

Soon, that trickle would turn into a flood.

Hopefully.

"Good afternoon," Emma said to the couple.

The couple said hello and walked through the store, browsing. Their dog was sniffing around, as if investigating a crime scene. It had a white coat with patches of brown and black hair.

Rugby laid in the path of the couple, and they both smiled at him. The beagle sniffed Rugby, who paid no mind to the small hound.

"Hey, big fella," the man said, his Georgian accent thick. It reminded Sarah of Marigold's accent.

The man bent down and let Rugby sniff his hand. He rubbed Rugby behind the ear.

"He's loving it," the woman said.

Rugby cocked his head, enjoying the massage.

"And what's your name?" the man said, still petting Rugby.

"His name's Rugby," Sarah said, walking over to the couple.

"Love that name."

Sarah smiled and pet the beagle, feeling its smooth coat. "Thanks. So, what's your dog's name?"

"Sherlock."

Sarah chuckled. "Do we have ourselves a sleuth?"

"He's always nosing into everything," the woman said. "Very inquisitive."

Just then, Sarah heard a scratching sound near the back of the store.

"What's that?" Sarah asked Emma.

"Oh darn," Emma said, hastily putting the last of the items on the shelf. "I keep forgetting Winston likes to take naps in Grandpa's office. And I'm used to closing doors..."

Emma rushed over and opened the office door.

Winston pranced out and made his way over to Sherlock.

"A corgi!" the woman said. "I just love corgis. Phil, I keep telling you—"

"—we should get a corgi," Phil said, finishing her sentence. "I know, Val...If you want, we should adopt one, then."

"What's her name?" Val asked.

"*His* name is Winston."

"If we get a corgi," Val said to Phil, "we should name it Watson."

Sarah smiled at the couple. She saw Emma picking up the empty box, shaking her head at the conversation.

Her cousin went to the back of the store to get another box to unload.

"That would be adorable," Sarah said, smirking. "Sherlock and Watson."

Winston and Sherlock sniffed one another, ignoring the humans who chatted above them. Rugby paid no mind to anybody, conked out from the relaxing massage. Misty, just as inquisitive as the hound, streaked past the canine trio. She didn't stop to investigate, though.

"So, are these two both yours?" Phil asked Sarah.

"Just the sleeping giant. The other one followed me home the other night."

"Oh my," Val said, petting Winston.

"Yeah, but I have flyers all around town. If you hear of anyone looking for their lost corgi, tell them to stop by here."

The couple finished petting the dogs. "Sure."

They strode around the store, Sherlock nearby, still investigating.

After they bought a few items, they left, and the boutique was silent once more.

"Sherlock and Watson," Emma muttered, rolling her eyes.

"What?" Sarah said, giving her cousin a look. "It's cute!"

PANIC AT THE PIER

"Whatever."

Larry rushed in. He carried a large serving plate filled with brownies.

"Special delivery!"

Sarah dug into the piping-hot brownies, taking her first bite. "Mmm."

"Store bought?" Emma asked, eyeing them suspiciously.

Larry looked shocked.

Emma smirked. "What? Did I strike a nerve?"

"No way these are store bought," Sarah said between bites.

"They aren't," Larry said. "Homemade, as usual."

Emma picked one up, eyeing it closer. "Uh-huh."

"These are up there with Fudderman's treats," Sarah said, onto her second brownie.

Larry's eyes lit up and he ignored Emma. "This is why you're my favorite granddaughter."

Emma gasped. "Hey!"

They chatted over brownies and the afternoon slipped by. A few customers came in, purchasing some small-ticket items. By the end of the day, after tallying up the total sales for the day, Sarah noted that her grandpa seemed pleased.

After closing up shop, they all went upstairs to the apartment.

Relaxation was on the agenda.

Misty swept by Larry's legs in the kitchen as he cooked up dinner.

Emma laid on the couch, a book in hand, with Winston nearby, napping.

Sarah joined her cousin in the living room, choosing her grandpa's recliner—the coziest spot in the apartment. She curled up and felt Rugby's large head on her lap. She ran a finger between his eyes and they closed slowly.

"What are you reading?" Sarah asked.

"Murder mystery."

"Any good?"

Emma huffed. "I'd like to find out, so…"

Sarah looked down at Rugby, his eyes still shut. "Sorry, Em."

Looking over at Emma, she saw the book was now flat down on her chest and her eyes were shut.

"What's wrong?" Sarah asked.

"I just keep thinking about everything that's going on."

"Don't worry about it."

"A potential killer is on the loose."

"A person of interest," Sarah corrected.

Emma's eyes opened. "But this—"

"You're jumping to conclusions again," Larry called from the kitchen.

"Maybe I am," Emma said. "But things just don't sit right..."

Sarah leaned back. "What do you want me to do about it?"

"Can you call Adam? Get the latest news. He's sweet on you."

"Yeah. But he would have told me by now if anything had changed. Or if they'd found Orloff."

It was true. Adam would have called her to tell her what was really going on. And she didn't want to be too pushy in calling him to find out.

Maybe nothing had changed.

Or maybe...

Sarah reached into her phone to check to see if she had any messages from Adam. She'd remembered to turn the phone's volume up but hadn't heard it ring.

When she pressed the side button on her phone, the device didn't light up.

"Hmm."

She tried again, but it still didn't work.

Getting up from the recliner, she stepped over to her backpack. She checked for her charger, but it wasn't in the bag.

She pulled on her sneakers and made her way toward the door.

"Where are you going?" Larry asked. "Dinner's almost ready."

"Out to my car quick. I think I left my phone charger out there."

A pot clanged as Larry drained the pasta into a colander in the sink. "Okay, I'll have the meatballs ready in a minute, so be quick."

"I will."

Rugby walked over to the door where Sarah stood. He looked up at her expectantly.

"Stay here, boy."

Sarah went out the door, car keys in hand.

She closed the door behind her and descended the stairs, then made her way out of the building. Once outside, she turned left and hurried along the sidewalk.

The moon wasn't as bright as the previous night, half concealed by clouds. She was glad that her grandpa had left an outside light on in front of the store. Perhaps he kept the light on to thwart any burglars who may have made a second attempt on his quaint boutique.

Sarah walked toward her car, which was parked past the Bait and Tackle shop. She usually liked to leave the parking spots directly outside the boutique open for their customers, and did the same for the friendly couple who owned the neighboring shop.

Beyond her car, she saw Larry's Pinto. A nearby streetlight revealed the hatchback sedan's lime green color.

She frowned, staring at the ancient relic. "I would've gone with any other color."

Unlocking her Corolla with the press of a button on her key fob, she heard the locking mechanism click.

She opened the passenger door, and the overhead cabin light illuminated the interior.

"There you are," she said, grabbing her charger from the passenger seat.

Closing the door, she pressed the key fob once again and heard the car chirp, confirming that it was indeed locked.

She half-turned when she spotted a hooded figure off to her right.

She gasped and froze, like her feet were cemented to the sidewalk.

Was it the burglar from the previous night?

Was he back to finish the deed?

Or perhaps it was the killer...

Seconds crept by and she wanted to run, but somehow her legs wouldn't work.

Quickly, the person pulled their hood back and she

saw the man's face. He was tall and had dark hair. But it was the raven tattoo on the side of his neck that made her gasp. The man looked upset, frazzled almost.

Before Sarah could say anything to the man, he turned and rushed into a doorway.

As the door closed slowly behind him, she could hear the man's boots echo in the stairwell as he ascended the steps to the second floor of the neighboring building.

"Is that…"

A wave of energy coursed through her as she had a flash of realization.

"Of course!"

Sarah raced back up to her grandpa's apartment, found the closest power outlet, and plugged her phone in.

In a matter of seconds, it had charged enough for her to power it on.

Sarah dialed Adam, her heart racing faster with each second she waited for him to answer.

"C'mon…c'mon…"

Finally, she heard his voice. It was groggy; she hoped she didn't wake him. Too bad, she thought. This is too important.

"Adam," she said, gripping the phone tighter. "You'll never believe who I just saw."

CHAPTER 11

"Who?" Adam asked, his voice still groggy.

"Orloff Minsky."

"Really? Where is he now?"

"He's back in his apartment, above the Bait and Tackle shop next door."

"I know where he lives," Adam said.

Of course, she realized. His apartment was probably the first place they looked for him.

"Thanks, Sarah," came Adam's voice again, disrupting her thoughts.

"You're welcome."

"And Sarah?"

"Yeah."

"Let me know if you see or hear anything else. Hopefully, once we question him, we'll have a better understanding of what happened."

"Sure," she said

After they said their goodbyes, Sarah hung up the phone and left it on the charger.

"Dinner's served," Larry said, placing a big bowl of pasta in the middle of the table. He rushed over to the kitchen and retrieved some plates, silverware, and napkins. There were already glasses of water on the table, and he asked, "Anyone want anything else to drink? Tea? Wine? Chocolate milk?"

"Chocolate milk?" Emma asked, sitting on the couch. She set her whodunit mystery novel on the coffee table and stood up. "We're not seven."

Larry carried over a bowl of meatballs in his secret tomato sauce and set it on the table. "Well, I have all of the above, so let me know."

"Water's fine," Emma said, lumbering over to the table.

"Sarah?"

"What?"

"What do you want to drink?" Larry asked, hesitating to sit down.

Sarah took a seat at the table and eyed up the glass of water. "You said wine?"

Larry smiled. "Let me tell you what I've got."

After selecting a bottle of wine, Larry poured two glasses.

"Sure you don't want any?" Larry asked Emma.

Emma was already serving herself. She squinted to look at the bottle of wine, and asked, "Is that a Dunham Vineyards label I see?"

Larry looked proud. "Sure is."

"No, thanks," Emma said, and she took a sip of water.

Resentment runs deep with Emma, Sarah thought. Marigold Dunham was a sweetheart as far as she was concerned, and she couldn't understand why Emma was so bitter toward her.

Larry brought two glasses over and set one by Sarah.

"So, anything going on, Sarah?"

"Well, I spotted Orloff out there—"

"You *what?*" Emma asked. "When?"

"When I was getting my charger. That's why I was calling Adam a minute ago. Didn't you hear me on the phone?"

"I've been in and out," Emma admitted. "Didn't get much sleep last night."

The screeching of brakes outside caught Sarah's attention.

"That's probably Adam now."

Emma rose from the table in a hurry and rushed to

the street-side picture window. Sarah followed her and saw her cousin's face pressed against the glass.

"No gawking," Sarah said.

"Oh, please."

Outside, Sarah could see two officers walking toward the entrance to Orloff's apartment.

Emma squinted. "Neither of them look like Adam."

"When I called him, he was groggy. He's probably off duty and just called it in."

"Makes sense."

They stood and waited for several minutes.

"Dinner's getting cold," came Larry's voice from the table.

Neither Sarah nor Emma paid any mind. They simply stood, waiting for confirmation that Orloff hadn't slipped away into the night before the authorities could find him.

Maybe Orloff was stopping by his apartment to get something he'd forgotten in his haste to get away. Sarah spotting him was likely the last thing he expected. Sarah shook her head, realizing that Emma was rubbing off on her. If she wasn't careful, she would assume the man was guilty of—

"Oh," Emma said, her voice wire-tight. "I think I see…there he is. Look at that scowl on Orloff's face."

Sarah leaned forward, getting a better look. So, the

man hadn't stopped by quickly only to disappear again. He was *willingly* going into the station, or so it seemed.

Just then, Orloff looked up at them, his green eyes practically boring through her. She rushed away from the window, and Emma followed suit.

"He's going to think we're creepers," Sarah said.

"I don't care what he thinks. Not after what he did."

Sarah stared at her cousin, dumbfounded.

"What?" Emma asked.

"You read whodunit novels a lot, right? You should know that they are simply taking him down to the station for questioning. Stop jumping—"

"—to conclusions. Got it," Emma said, nodding, then made her way back over to the table. She twirled some spaghetti on her fork and swooped it up into her mouth. One last string of spaghetti was still hanging halfway down her chin by the time Sarah reached the table. Emma sucked the pasta in, making an obnoxious slurping sound.

"So, about you not being seven," Larry said, shaking his head. "I don't believe it."

Sarah was taking a sip of wine when she heard Larry's jab, and it took all the restraint she could muster not to spit it out in a fit of laughter.

Larry raised his glass again, looking at Sarah.

"To the police getting one step closer to solving this case," Sarah said.

She raised her glass and heard the *clink* sound when it tapped against Larry's. She took a sip of wine and hoped that the case would be put to bed before the tourist season started up. It was vital to the well-being of the residents and business owners of Cascade Cove that it returned to its normal, idyllic state.

After dinner, they settled in for the night.

Larry allowed Sarah to enjoy his recliner while he sat at the dining room table, paging through one of Grandma's scrapbooks.

She sat there, cell phone fully charged and nearby.

Emma was back on the couch, getting toward the end of her mystery story.

Leaning back in the chair, Sarah thought about the hooded man who'd tried breaking in the previous night. Then she thought of the way Orloff was dressed in the same black hoodie.

Her brow furrowed.

None of it made any sense.

Why would their neighbor try to break into their shop?

For that matter, why would *anyone* try to break into a mom-and-pop pet boutique in a sleepy seaside town during what was technically still the off-season? Adam had said a burglar would be after the cash in the register, but during the off-season, they wouldn't have much money at all.

Then her mind focused on the fact that Orloff had been fired the day before Jacobs' body was found.

Maybe he was the killer—he certainly had the motive...

Though there were still many unanswered questions that nagged at her.

Soon, she'd find out from Adam about what they learned while questioning their prime suspect. She checked that her phone wasn't accidentally on its silent mode. She wouldn't want to miss that call.

Until then, all she could do was wait.

It was going to be a long night.

CHAPTER 12

The next morning, Sarah awoke to her cell phone's ringtone. She reached to the night-stand and grabbed her phone. The caller ID showed Adam's name and face.

Sarah answered the call in a hurry.

"What happened with Orloff?" Sarah asked, getting right to the point. Thinking about it had kept her up most of the night, and she was dying to know all of the details.

"We just released him."

"What?" Sarah said, her voice louder. On the single bed next to hers, Emma turned in her sleep.

Sarah got out of her bed and rushed out of the room, as to not disturb her cousin any more.

"It wasn't him," Adam said.

PANIC AT THE PIER

"Are you sure?"

"Yeah. He claims he was at his weekly poker night, got there around nine o'clock at night, at least three hours before the time of death. We have half a dozen guys who corroborated his story, so…"

"Hmm."

"Yeah."

"So are we back to it being an accident, or—"

"I wish that were the case. We're officially in homicide territory now."

Sarah dropped the phone to the floor. She scrambled to pick it back up.

"Sorry, Adam. Did you say homicide?"

"Yeah. Not only do we have the signs of a struggle, we found blood and—"

"Where?"

"At his residence—Jacobs Manor."

"In his house, or—"

"It was outside. Listen, we discovered it the morning his body was found. Long story short, we've confirmed that it was indeed Jacobs' blood, and not somebody else's, or an animal's."

"So, if it wasn't Orloff, then who do you think it could be?"

"I'm not sure, but we'll be questioning as many people as we can. Mr. Minsky was the most-likely suspect. With him exonerated, we'll be going down our list."

"Oh my…" Sarah said.

The silence on the other end lingered for a moment, then Adam asked, "Have you heard anything else through the grapevine?"

"You mean…"

"I know how gossip goes in the Cove. And I know that your grandpa is among the most popular people in the area. Since you're his granddaughter…well, let's just say, people trust you. Are more comfortable with you."

"Do you want me to use my secret ninja skills?"

"I was thinking more your people skills, being a teacher and quasi-caseworker."

Sarah was hesitant to answer. This was no longer a case where an accident was the probable cause with the signs of struggle being misconstrued "evidence." Now, there was more solid evidence by the day, and a killer was most certainly on the loose. This fact made her wonder if she should even get involved—helping the police in any way could put her family in grave danger.

But she knew that Adam needed her help. It was common knowledge that not everyone liked talking to the cops. Now, someone like her, whom everyone in the town had known since she was just a little girl…they would trust and confide in her.

She could make a difference and help get justice for the murder of that crazy old coot, Mr. Jacobs. Not to mention, if she acted quickly, she could help to bring a sense of normalcy back to Cascade Cove before the summer season began. She was sure a Murder Town wouldn't be at the top of vacationers' list of destinations. If this case dragged on, the summer would surely be a bust, and her grandpa's boutique...well, this might be the straw that broke that quaint little mom-and-pop shop to pieces.

"Are you still there?" Adam asked.

"Yeah. Are you sure about this?"

"Yeah, but again, if you help, you'll need to be discreet."

"I'll do it. Cascade Cove means the world to me, and I'll do whatever I can to help you catch the killer."

"Thanks, Sarah. Call me with any info you find."

"Will do."

They finished their call, and she slid the phone into the pocket of her pajamas.

She felt a presence behind her and turned around.

Emma stood there, slack-jawed.

"How much of that did you hear?"

Sarah knew she didn't even have to ask.

"So who are we going to question first?" Emma asked Sarah, pouring a bowl of cereal. She opened the fridge and pulled out a carton of milk, pouring it over the cereal.

"I'm not sure yet," Sarah said.

"Well, who has any sort of motive?"

"Jacobs was a landlord, and had just raised his rent, so that means any of his tenants had motive."

"Yeah, we know Patricia Greensmith was a tenant—"

"She has a solid alibi…"

"I know," Emma said, "but who else is a tenant of Jacobs?"

"Henry Fudderman, but remember, he was at his nephew's grad party that night."

Larry stepped into the kitchen, stretching as he poured himself a cup of coffee. "Won first place," he said, then took a sip of his coffee and plodded off to another part of the apartment.

"Grandpa's in his own little world today," Emma said. "Wait till he finds out about everything we know…"

"Hold off on telling him. Let him enjoy the morning without fear of a killer on the loose."

Emma nodded.

"So Patricia Greensmith, Henry Fudderman, and Orloff Minsky are all cleared. Who else is there?"

"We'll have to make a list, then go walk around to talk to people."

"Yeah," Sarah said. "But we need to be discreet. We can't raise any suspicions that we're helping the police at all. Remember, people will talk to us because they like us, trust us, and have known us since we were little."

"Right. We'll be like ninjas."

Sarah rolled her eyes, realizing she and her cousin were two peas in the same pod.

After breakfast, Sarah and Emma met Larry in the boutique. He was sorting the display of bowties and waved at them as they walked in. At the other side of the boutique, Rugby and Winston were causing a ruckus, and Misty dodged them as they played.

"So, it's confirmed," Larry said, forehead glazed with sweat. "A killer's on the loose in Cascade Cove."

Larry stepped over to the counter and grabbed a donut off a plate, taking a bite.

"How did you find out so quickly?" Sarah asked.

"I wasn't open more than fifteen minutes before Henry Fudderman rushed in to give me the news. He also brought us some donuts, on the house." He lifted the donut.

"Word spreads quickly around here," Emma said. "Is that a Cascade Cruller?"

"Sure is," Larry said, still chewing. "You want one?"

"No, thanks," Emma said. "Sarah and I are going out on the town a bit."

Larry's brows furrowed. "Emma, you promised to cover for me while I run errands today."

Emma huffed. "Oh yeah, I forgot."

"Looks like I'll be going alone, then," Sarah said, eyeing up the donuts. She grabbed a cruller and ate it in only five bites.

"Well, be careful out there, Sarah," Larry said.

"Grandpa, it's daytime. And I'll just be around Cascade Cove. Police are on high-alert, no doubt. I'll be fine."

Sarah strolled out of the boutique, waving goodbye to her grandpa and cousin. Outside, more and more shopkeepers were preparing their stores for the coming weekend—the beginning of the season.

Sarah waved to Henry Fudderman, who stood outside his bakery.

"Did your grandpa relay what I told him?" Henry called from across the street.

"Yeah," Sarah called back.

"Be careful."

"I will."

Sarah continued along, passing by Patricia's Tea Room.

"Don't have to worry about Patricia," Sarah muttered to herself.

She walked along, though none of the businesses on that end were open yet, so there was nobody to question.

She realized she should have gone the other way first. She could have stopped in at Gordy's Deli or stopped to see Kacey. Neither had any motive she could think of, though both could have given her some leads. Right now, she didn't have much.

But there was a reason she came this way first. There was something she had to check out.

Sarah saw the beginning of an old wrought iron fence off to her right. She continued walking along the fence. The house beyond was foreboding, but that was mostly because Sarah knew its significance.

"Jacobs Manor," she said.

Sarah sighed. Beyond the house was the pier. The same pier she remembered seeing the police at when she first came into town and was sitting on the boardwalk behind Patricia's Tea Room.

The place was huge up close, and the property equally vast. She wondered how they found the small spot of blood—would have been like finding a needle in a haystack.

"I wonder what happened here..."

There was no way to know, but Sarah figured whoever offed Jacobs did it at his house. Perhaps the murderer knocked Jacobs over the head. Then they carted him off to the pier, inadvertently leaving a little bit of blood behind. From the pier, they dumped his body, probably thinking it would wash away with the tide. The fishermen then found his body. Her guesstimate of the timeline of events was a probable scenario.

Sarah looked around. On either side of the road, there were other houses past the Jacobs estate, though there was not a soul in sight. This coming weekend, however, these houses would be rented by all of the tourists who would, hopefully, flock to town. Now, the scene was as quiet and eerie as a graveyard in the middle of the night.

She thought of knocking on the doors of some of the houses, especially the place across the street from Jacobs Manor. Then she thought it would be futile for now—all of the houses looked empty—no cars anywhere.

Besides that, something just didn't feel right. Perhaps she shouldn't be out this way all by herself, especially with a killer on the loose...

Sarah turned and walked back, intent on talking

with a few people past where her grandpa's place was. On the way, she saw a man in a hoodie leaning against one of the buildings.

Sarah slowed her pace, apprehensive.

The man looked familiar…

Was it really him?

Sarah's voice came out as a mere whisper: "Orloff?"

CHAPTER 13

The man stood looking blankly out into the street. His face was a mask, and the fact that Sarah couldn't read him disturbed her.

Was it Orloff?

After seeing the raven tattoo, she was certain it was.

Stepping closer toward him, she kept reminding herself that he'd been exonerated. Solid alibi.

Still, she was uneasy.

She was tempted to try to avoid him completely, so she looked to her right into the street. Out of the corner of her eye, she realized he was staring at her.

On his face, she noticed a flash of recognition. "Sorry if I frightened you last night," he said.

Sarah slowed her pace even more and turned to look at him. He now seemed kind. Maybe she was too wrapped up in her own imagination of who she thought he was that she hadn't even given him a fair chance.

"Oh, yeah. No worries."

Now was her chance to talk to him. Get more information about what he knew. Though she was sure Adam would have told her any key information gleaned from his questioning, it was possible that Orloff had forgotten to mention something of importance to the authorities, either accidentally or deliberately.

"I'm Sarah, by the way."

"Nice to meet you, Sarah. I've seen you around the pet boutique. I'm Orloff."

Sarah saw a police cruiser pass them and sighed.

"A lot of stuff going on lately," Sarah said.

"I'll say."

"Sorry we were gawking out the window last night—police activity is a rare thing around these parts."

"Don't worry about it. I'm used to gawkers. I'm the only Russian in this town."

"How long have you been here?"

"A few months."

"Do you like it here?"

"It's nice, when I'm not hounded by the cops."

"Yeah," Sarah said, trying to read the guy's body language, but he stayed oddly neutral. Perhaps it was just the way he normally behaved, or maybe there was more to it.

"Why were they hounding you?"

"Oh, it was something dealing with my ex-boss, Mr. Jacobs. If you hadn't heard, the old man has kicked up the daisies. Or is it 'petunias'? Well, he's kicking up some sort of flower now…"

Sarah's heart beat a little faster. The way he talked about Jacobs' demise, without a hint of emotion, bothered her. Still, she had to dig a little deeper.

"I heard about that," she said. "Were they questioning you?"

Orloff nodded.

"Why?"

"Like I said, I used to work for Mr. Jacobs. Apparently, you can't get fired from a job now without being suspected of something."

"Well, you have to admit, the timing was a bit odd."

Orloff raised an eyebrow. "Coincidences happen. This was one of them."

"Yeah. So where were you that night?"

"To be honest, I was losing my shirt."

It was Sarah's turn to raise an eyebrow. "I don't…"

"Poker night."

Sarah nodded. So is that why Orloff looked so upset, even before the police took him in for questioning? He was probably still brooding over the fact he'd not only lost his job, but lost money playing poker as well.

"Sorry to hear that," Sarah said.

Orloff looked at Sarah. "Was up big, then lost it all, plus some. Stupid of me, though; I just lost my job. Oh well."

A bright yellow Beetle passed by them on the street, and Orloff glanced at it. Then his brows furrowed.

Sarah said, "What's wrong?"

"That car."

"What about it?"

"That yellow Bug...I think I saw that car before."

"Where?"

"It was parked outside Mr. Jacobs' place when I was walking to poker."

"The night of his death?"

Orloff nodded.

"Did you tell the cops?"

Orloff shook his head. "I didn't think of it. They only asked where I was and who was there that could corroborate my story."

"Do you know what time you saw it?"

Orloff considered her question. "Hmm. A little before nine. We start the first hand at nine, and I was running a little late."

"Are you sure?"

"Yeah. The sun hadn't quite set yet. And I remember looking at my watch once I arrived to the game, and it was exactly nine o'clock then. I only remember because the guys were giving me a hard time because they were already dealing."

"I see."

"And I also…" he started, face scrunched up.

"What?" Sarah asked.

"I don't know. It might be nothing."

Another car zipped by them, the sound of its engine loud in Sarah's ears. She waited until the sound faded away, then asked, "What?"

"On my way to poker that night, past where Jacobs Manor is, I saw a small dog roaming around."

"A small dog?"

"Yeah. Little fellow, about this big." Orloff used his hands to describe the size of the dog. "I didn't think anything of it, figured it belonged to one of the residents or someone on vacation…"

Sarah's chest tensed. "What kind of dog?"

"Hmm. It was short and long…mostly brown, with perky ears…"

Sarah pulled a copy of her flyer from her back pocket, unfolded the paper, and showed it to Orloff.

"Did it look like this?"

Orloff stared down at the flyer, studying the picture of Winston.

"It was hard to see, with all the late-day shadows, so I can't be sure..." Orloff studied the picture. "Hmm, did kind of look like—"

Orloff's phone suddenly rang. He pulled the phone from his pocket and checked it. "Need to take this."

"Okay," Sarah said. "See you later, Orloff."

Orloff answered his call, nodding at Sarah as he started talking in Russian to the person who'd called him.

Sarah continued along, feeling her heartbeat pounding in her chest. The fact Orloff had seen Winston made sense. The little dog had come from the part of town where Jacobs Manor was. It could have wandered past the old man's house, having nothing to do with the incident that night. Or maybe there was more to it...

Then her mind drifted back to the yellow Beetle parked outside Jacobs' house that night. That, too, could be merely coincidental, though she knew she had to figure out who that bright yellow car belonged to.

She strode back to the mid-way section of the main strip and hurried over to her grandpa's shop.

Inside, she saw Emma behind the counter.

Emma looked up from her laptop. "There you are!"

"Where's Grandpa?"

"He's gallivanting around town in his old rust-bucket. So where did you go so far?"

"Walked out to Jacobs Manor."

"Oh yeah?"

"Yeah, it's like a ghost town out that way."

"It's pre-peak...that'll be hopping soon," Emma said, now staring into her laptop, mesmerized. Her fingers tapped lightly on the keyboard as she typed.

"Yeah."

"So, what else did you find out?" Emma asked, still fixated on her computer.

"I ran into Orloff."

Emma looked up at Sarah, no longer typing.

"Go on..."

"He said he saw Winston the night of the murder, out past Jacobs Manor. It was at least three hours before the time of Jacobs' death."

"I see."

"And Orloff said he saw a yellow Beetle."

"A yellow Beetle?"

"Yeah, this brand-new, bright yellow Beetle that drove past us."

"Hmm."

"Orloff's face was unreadable until he saw that Beetle. Turns out he saw the Beetle parked outside Jacobs Manor several hours before the murder."

"So Winston and a yellow Beetle..."

"Yeah, I'm sure Winston is a pure coincidence, but I want to find out who owns that yellow Beetle."

Sarah picked up the last Cascade Cruller from the Fudderman's box and took a bite. She continued, "I'm going to scope out the town a bit more. See if I can track it down."

"Don't forget to check over at the strip mall," Emma said.

"Good idea." She finished the last of her Cruller. "Okay, I'll be back in a little bit."

On her way out, a customer walked in, a pug by their side.

Sarah walked by them and nodded, then strode out the door, Emma's greeting—"Welcome to Larry's Pawfect Boutique!"—barely audible with the street sounds filling Sarah's ears.

She walked past the Bait and Tackle shop and then turned right to traverse the road. When she didn't see any oncoming traffic, she stepped out to cross the street. While in the middle of the road, she stopped and scanned the main strip. It was straight as an arrow, and so she peered in both directions. A bright yellow car would have stuck out like a sore thumb if parked on that street, though she didn't see any cars of that color.

On the other side of the road, she made her way to a

side street. Down that way was the largest grocery store in town, located at the end of a strip mall. It wasn't on the town's main road, though it was still within walking distance. Sarah wanted to check it out to see what she could find, since the store's parking lot was large, and she crossed her fingers that she'd see that car coming or going.

After a half-mile walk, she saw the store's parking lot off in the distance.

During peak season, there wasn't usually an empty parking spot to be found in the lot, but now, it was only a quarter full.

Stepping closer, she scanned the parking lot and it didn't take long for her to spot the yellow Beetle parked near the store's entrance.

Hurrying along, she saw that the car was empty.

Whoever owned the Beetle was still in the store.

Sarah walked up to the front of the store, watching a few people with shopping carts leaving the place. None approached the yellow car. She sat on one of the benches outside and leaned back.

Hopefully it wouldn't take long for the car's owner to emerge.

But when they did, she was certain she'd have her next lead.

A half hour passed, and Sarah's back was beginning to hurt. She stared at the yellow Beetle intently, as if it would help its owner emerge from the grocery store.

What if the person wasn't in the store, after all? Perhaps they parked here for the day and walked to the beach.

Sarah pulled her phone from her pocket and texted Emma, utilizing her phone's talk-to-text feature: "Found the car."

Emma replied in a matter of seconds: "And???"

"No owner in sight. Waiting outside the grocery store now."

"Keep me posted!"

"Okay."

Sarah pocketed her phone and looked up. There, she saw a woman standing at the side of the Beetle, loading groceries into the back seat.

The woman's back was turned to Sarah, but something about the woman's clothing was familiar.

Sarah stayed seated, anticipating a glimpse of the woman's face at any moment.

The woman finished putting the groceries in her car, and when she returned the cart to the front of the store, Sarah got a good look at her face.

"Could it be..."

Though the woman was wearing big sunglasses and her hat shaded much of her face, Sarah was certain she knew exactly who this woman was.

"Uh..." Sarah started, but the woman was quick to return her cart and rush off toward her Beetle before Sarah could get another word out, or even mutter her name.

Not in the mood for small talk, Sarah thought. But she also noted the hurried way in which the woman walked. Something about it wasn't quite right.

The woman sped off, and Sarah fished her phone out of her pocket in a hurry.

"You'll never guess who it is," Sarah said into her phone, watching her words quickly appear on the screen.

"Who???" came the reply.

Sarah took a deep breath and smiled. She knew this revelation would make Emma's day.

CHAPTER 14

*B*efore she could mutter the woman's name into her phone, Sarah saw that she was receiving a call from Emma.

Sarah answered the call in one ring. "Impatient, are we?"

"Just tell me," came Emma's voice.

"You'll never believe this. The yellow Beetle belongs to Marigold."

"Marigold Dunham?"

"Yeah."

"I knew it. So I was right about her after all."

Sarah pulled the phone away to save her eardrums. "I was going to talk to Marigold," Sarah said, "but she sped off before I could pick my jaw up off the sidewalk."

"Hold on," Emma said. "Grandpa's calling me on the other line. Hopefully he's not broken down again."

Sarah rose from the bench and started off into the parking lot.

"I'm on my way back. I'll talk to you then."

They hung up and she hurried through the parking lot, along a side road, and found herself back on the main strip. It only took another five minutes before she reached the boutique.

Inside, Sarah saw Emma still sitting at the counter.

"Is Grandpa okay?" Sarah asked.

Emma nodded. "Yeah, he just got back and is in the office finishing up some paperwork. Just needed me to remind him what the password is to get into the admin for the website. Anyway, that's crazy about Marigold. I knew she'd be up to no good."

"Why do you say that?"

"Didn't you know? She's the town debutante. Born with a silver spoon in her mouth."

"I kind of gathered that. But she's nice."

"Yeah, well, you know that her family owns the vineyard, the ranch…"

Sarah nodded.

"That was all passed down to her, but—"

A light went on in Sarah's head. "The soil contamination."

"Bingo. So now she's struggling."

"But what does that have to do with Mr. Jacobs?"

"Let me finish," Emma said, rising from her stool. Sarah noted how chipper Emma now was, like when she'd first seen her upon arriving to Cascade Cove.

"Okay."

"Let's just say 'Marigold-digger' didn't get that nickname on a whim. She's known to chase after wealthy men. And as we know, Jacobs was a wealthy man."

"But he's old enough to be her father..." Sarah paused. "Or grandfather, for that matter."

"Your point?"

"So you think her possible motive is financial gain?"

Emma nodded. "Born rich, and now gradually losing her wealth...It's a great setup for her to dig some wealth out of the ole Jacobs coffers."

"Okay, that's an interesting theory and all, but it begs the question, why would she want him dead? It doesn't make sense."

Scratching her cheek, Emma pondered the question. Then her face lit up. "I think Jacobs was married."

"Really? Who?"

"Oh, I can't remember her name," she said, snapping her fingers. Then she turned toward the office. "Grandpa!"

Larry's head popped out from around the door frame of his office. "What's up, Emma?"

"What's Jacob's wife's name?"

"Charlotte. What a sweet, sweet woman. I wonder how she's holding up...I heard she's been so upset."

Emma yelled back to their grandpa, "Yeah, you should probably send her flowers or a card or something."

"Oh, dear heavens! You're right." Larry disappeared into his office. "I should call a florist or something. What an awful neighbor I am."

Emma looked at Sarah, seemingly proud of herself.

Sarah narrowed her eyes at her cousin. "How come I haven't heard of Charlotte?"

"I don't know. They've been married for a few years now. Maybe if you visited more..."

Sarah rolled her eyes. "You couldn't remember her name!"

"That's because she's very private. Of what I heard, she only runs with her own crowd."

"What crowd is that?"

"The rich kind, and just like her husband, she's hardly seen on the boardwalk, especially in the summer when it's crowded with tourists."

"So wouldn't Marigold want *Charlotte* out of the

picture if she wanted to get to Jacobs and his money? Why murder Jacobs?"

Emma grimaced. "Hmm. Good point. Maybe she was mad because Jacobs wouldn't leave his wife, and so she killed him? Or maybe she *was* trying to kill Charlotte to get her out of the picture, and instead, accidentally killed Jacobs..."

"Sounds like an episode of *Murder, She Wrote.*"

Emma furrowed her brows. "What's that?"

Sarah shook her head. "Never mind. So, you're thinking maybe Marigold and Jacobs were having an affair?"

"Yeah, it's certainly possible. And she has a motive, since he's wealthy..."

Sarah considered that, then said, "Wouldn't the rumor mill churn with that juicy tidbit? If they were having an affair, wouldn't that be the talk of the town?"

"I suppose so. I don't know, then."

Sarah shrugged. "We'll have to go talk to Marigold."

"Then why don't you go over and see if she's there at her wine shop?"

"It's down almost to the other end of the boardwalk," Sarah said. "Are you sure?"

"Yeah, I have to watch the front of the store while grandpa finishes up stuff in his office and I can't wait."

"Alright then." Sarah exited the store and walked briskly down the main road toward the Dunham Vineyards outlet. It was a small hole-in-the-wall place that served merely as a front for the vast operation that was inland, an hour drive or so.

Once at the wine outlet, Sarah saw the CLOSED sign.

"Closed for the season."

Perhaps it would open up sooner than later, with the summer months nearly upon them. Surely Marigold wouldn't miss those prime months if she were struggling with money. Or, perhaps, the contaminated soil issue devastated their crop so much that there wouldn't be any product to sell this year.

Either way, she'd have to figure out another way to find Marigold and her bright yellow Beetle again.

As she walked back to the store, she scanned the street. Down the main strip, she saw a yellow vehicle roar toward her, but frowned when she saw it wasn't a Beetle.

"Where are you, Marigold?"

Across the street, she hurried along the sidewalk and back to her grandpa's.

Emma was straightening up when she entered.

"That was fast," Emma said. "I take it she wasn't there."

"Nope. Closed for the season."

"So now what?"

"I don't know. Do you know her number?"

Emma chortled.

"Well then," Sarah continued, "I guess we just cross our fingers we'll spot her car—or maybe she'll come in here to shop."

Later that night, Sarah sat in the recliner in her grandpa's apartment. She couldn't stop her mind from reeling about Marigold and the yellow Beetle. The rest of the day had been a bust, as far as spotting Marigold was concerned.

Emma was on the couch in her usual spot.

"Is that a new book?" Sarah asked.

"Yeah."

"How was the other one you just read?"

"Good. The murderer ended up being the last person I expected."

Sarah nodded and heard Rugby and Winston rush from the bedroom, Misty chasing after them. She went to the floor and sat with legs crossed. Petting the dogs, a thought suddenly struck her.

"Least-likely suspect?"

"Yeah, at least it was the person I suspected the least. Kept me guessing till the end. Gotta love a good page-turner like that."

"Hmm…" Sarah started.

"What?" Emma asked, eyeing up Sarah. She sat up and placed the book on the coffee table.

"Right now, it seems that Marigold doesn't have much of a motive."

"Not unless—"

"Unless she had something going on behind the scenes with Jacobs."

"She's a gold-digger," Emma said. "There's her motive. Money. Clear as day."

"But we don't *know* that she and Jacobs had a thing, much less knew each other."

"Everyone knows everyone else in this town. I guarantee she knew him. Besides, remember when we saw her at Patricia's Tea Room?"

"Yeah."

"She was the one who brought up Jacobs."

"That's right. She was pretty blunt in saying Jacobs drowned. I didn't think of it at the time, but looking back, that was rather odd."

"Misdirection," Emma said. "She was trying to plant something in our heads, and saying it was a drowning, she'd let us fill in the blanks and assume it was an accident."

"And don't forget—when we asked about *when* it happened, she left quickly to some appointment she said she was going to be late for."

"Didn't want to talk about Jacobs...just wanted to plant a seed that he drowned, *accidentally*, and let us stoke the rumor mill, helping her to cover up what really happened."

"But the rumor mill is saying it's a murder now..."

Emma scoffed. "That sneaky woman is clearly confident that nobody suspects her. By skipping town, she would probably figure that would make her look even *more* suspicious. She's a master of deception, don't forget that."

Sarah pondered this. Usually this was one of those times when Sarah would tell Emma not to jump to conclusions, but they had to be on to something. They had an idea of what her motive would be, considering her history and the fact she was gradually losing her wealth.

They were also almost certain that she knew Jacobs, and, according to Orloff, her car had been parked outside of Jacobs Manor only hours before the reported time-of-death.

So she most certainly had the opportunity to kill the old man, and the means.

But still, Sarah had to confirm the fact that she'd indeed known Jacobs. Right now, they were trying to connect dots without solid evidence. Some digging around town was in order.

"Tomorrow," Sarah said, "you and I will go around town and get to the bottom of this."

Emma's eyes lit up. "And with any luck, we'll find Marigold Dunham."

Sarah's eyes flew open, and she reached for her phone. It lay face-down on the nightstand by her bed. The glow of the screen nearly blinded her, and it took a second for her eyes to adjust.

"Two o'clock," she said, groggily.

Almost the witching hour.

Her throat was dry and so she stumbled out of bed and shuffled across the bedroom. Out in the kitchen, she got a glass from the cupboard and ran the tap for a moment, then swung her glass underneath.

Once full, she took a gulp of water and sighed.

She carried her glass into the living room. A single

lamp was on in the corner of the room. Off somewhere in the house, she heard someone snoring softly.

She sat on the recliner and placed the cup of water on the table next to the chair.

Why had she awoken so suddenly?

Perhaps her subconscious was trying to work through the problem again.

She took another sip of water, then rose from the chair and walked over to her grandpa's bookshelf. She ran her fingers along the spines of the scrapbooks and chose one.

"This should help put me to sleep."

She carried one of the scrapbooks over to the chair and sat down. Paging through, she looked at one old picture after another. Then she saw a few pictures that were actually in color. There were some pictures of the ocean and a couple of the pier. They looked to be more recent.

Turning the page, she froze.

She saw a woman's smiling face below a brimmed hat, the pier behind her.

Maybe that was the same pier behind Jacobs Manor...

To the woman's left, she saw a man who looked to be at least thirty years the woman's senior. He looked pensively into the camera, his lips straight across like he was on the verge of frowning.

Sarah leaned closer to the picture and studied it.

Beneath the picture, she saw her grandma's cursive writing. It took her a moment to decipher it.

"My goodness," Sarah said, then read the caption aloud: "John Jacobs and Marigold Dunham."

CHAPTER 15

The next morning, Sarah awoke to an alarm she had set on her phone. It took her about an hour to get showered and ready for her day, and once finished, she came out and smelled the sweet aroma of French toast. Larry's famous French toast was made with a fresh French bread loaf with cinnamon, powdered sugar, maple syrup, and usually pecans or walnuts. Regardless of the type of nut he decided to garnish it with this morning, she couldn't wait to dig in.

Emma was already up and at the table, nibbling on her breakfast.

Larry was bright-eyed, wearing one of his Hawaiian shirts. "Fresh off the griddle," he said. "And there's pure maple syrup over there."

Sarah got a few pieces of French toast and drizzled maple syrup on top.

"Emma," Sarah said between bites. "When will you be ready to go?"

"Where are you two going?" Larry asked.

Sarah looked over to her grandpa. "To talk to someone."

"Ah," Larry said. He flipped a few pieces of French toast on the griddle and smiled at the sizzling sound they made.

"Will you be okay at the shop while we're gone?" Emma asked.

"Should be fine."

"If not," Emma said, chewing, "just let us know."

"Sounds good. So, any word on Winston's owner?" Larry asked.

Sarah shook her head. "Haven't gotten a single call about it. I'm thinking of putting an ad in the local gazette, as well as the newspapers of the neighboring towns."

Emma looked up from her plate. "You think he wandered from another town? They are miles away…"

"Wouldn't hurt to try."

"The newspapers sell advertising space through their web sites now, so you can pay right online," Larry said. "What will they think of next?"

Emma rolled her eyes. "Yeah, but I think the gazette here in town hasn't jumped on the technological bandwagon yet."

Sarah looked at her cousin. "We'll have to stop by their office in town."

Emma pressed her fork down into her final piece of French toast and popped it into her mouth, smiling. "Roger that."

"So, Emma," Sarah said. "You've got to see this…"

Sarah walked over to the bookshelf and grabbed the scrapbook. She carried it over to the table and opened it to the photo of Marigold and John Jacobs.

Pointing at the photo, Sarah said, "Check this out."

Emma looked down at the photo and gasped. "So she *did* know him. Maybe our 'affair' theory is true after all."

"Is that who you're going to talk to today? That woman?" Larry asked.

Sarah hesitated, then nodded.

Larry ate his food, not speaking his mind, though Sarah could tell he was piecing things together. "Just be careful," was all he said. "Stay in public places."

"We will," Sarah said.

"Well, what are we waiting for? Let's go track her down and fill in some of the blanks." Emma reached over to the scrapbook and peeled the picture of

Marigold and Jacobs out from the old scrapbook. "And we'll take this with us, just in case."

After breakfast, Larry took Rugby, Winston, and Misty down to the boutique to get settled in before opening the store, and Sarah and Emma started off for a day on the town to search for Marigold Dunham.

They stopped at the local gazette's office, and Sarah filled out the requisite information and paid the fee for the ad. Only time would tell if Winston's rightful owners came forward to claim him. Afterward, they wandered about, asking any friendly face they stumbled upon if they'd seen Marigold.

They stopped in to see Gordy, getting some free slices of meat and cheese. He said he'd seen Marigold the previous day, but hadn't seen her since.

At Surf's Up, Isabella and Faye were working the shop as usual, their mother out sick due to feeling under the weather. Both said Marigold hadn't stepped foot in their establishment in months. "Not her cup of tea," they said. It was probably true—none of the accessories nor attire appeared to be her style.

And at the Banana Hammock Bar and Grill, Kacey told them it had been at least a few days since she'd seen her.

Outside the Bar and Grill, Sarah saw a yellow Beetle pulling in to the parking lot.

Emma smiled. "Well, who do we have here…"

"Let me do the talking," Sarah said.

Emma shrugged.

They strode down into the parking lot, and Sarah saw that the driver had parked. Out stepped Marigold, and she sauntered toward the restaurant.

"Hi, Marigold," Sarah said.

Emma waved but said nothing.

Marigold's smile looked plastic. "Good afternoon, ladies."

"Another nice day, isn't it?" Sarah said, trying to make small talk before she started her digging.

"Beautiful. I almost feel guilty sitting in a restaurant for an hour."

"Yeah," Sarah said.

Emma stayed quiet. Good.

Sarah quickly filled in the silence: "So have you heard anything else about what happened to Jacobs?"

"Nothing new. Apparently, it was a drowning. An accident. Open-and-shut case."

Sarah eyed Emma for a brief moment. The whole talk of the town was that this was now considered a homicide with a killer on the loose. She wondered how Marigold still considered it a case of accidental drowning.

"That's not what I heard," Sarah said. "Apparently,

they're saying there was foul play. They even took Orloff Minsky in for questioning. He had a solid alibi, but—"

"Listen, I don't want to talk about this," Marigold spat.

"Do you—"

"I said, I don't have anything to say to you about this. Now, if you'll excuse me, I—"

Emma cut in, "Orloff said he saw your car parked outside Jacobs Manor the night of the murder and—"

"Emma, stop," Sarah said, shooting her cousin a look.

So much for charm and discretion...

Marigold's face turned beet red. "I don't have to stand for these accusations—"

Emma raised her voice. "You knew Jacobs. Admit it."

"Please, that's enough," Sarah said to Emma, but it was too late.

Emma had already reached into her pocket and pulled out the picture of Marigold and John Jacobs standing side by side. She held it up toward Marigold. "You knew him," Emma said. "Here you are with him."

"Are you accusing me of—"

"No," Sarah cut in, "of course not. We're not accusing you of anything. We're just curious about—"

"If you have to know," Marigold said above Sarah,

voice firm, "I was with Charlotte that evening. Now, if you'll excuse me, I'd like to get on with my day."

Marigold stormed off. By the time Sarah turned around to watch the woman rush away, she had already entered the Bar and Grill, door closing behind her.

Sarah and Emma gawked at each other.

Emma was the first the speak: "Did Marigold just say she was *with Charlotte* the night John Jacobs was killed?"

CHAPTER 16

"*Y*eah, that's what she said," Sarah said, stepping away from the restaurant and back out to the main strip. "So Marigold was with John Jacobs' wife, Charlotte, the night of the murder…"

Emma strode by her side, silent.

They both walked slowly, minds spinning from the new information.

Then Emma spoke up, "So we should probably swing by Jacobs Manor to talk to Charlotte."

Sarah's chest tensed. "Yeah."

"What's wrong?"

Sarah thought of the foreboding house and the creepy feeling she got when she was there last, standing outside the wrought-iron gate. She thought of the fact that a murder had likely taken place there. But she had a mission, and Charlotte Jacobs was the next puzzle piece —she needed to be questioned.

"Nothing," Sarah said, finally. "Next stop: Jacobs Manor."

They forged on, walking past Larry's Pawfect Boutique with not much more than a glance, set on getting to the bottom of the mystery of what exactly happened to John Jacobs.

Before long, the wrought-iron fence came into view. They continued on until they reached the main gate. The gate was open, so they walked along the driveway and toward the house.

At the door, Sarah lifted the large knocker to rap on the door several times.

They waited for half a minute, though to Sarah it felt like an hour.

Behind them, a car drove by and then was gone.

She could hear the sound of waves crashing on the other side of the house.

Sarah knocked a second time, and then they waited once again.

"Nobody's home," Emma said, and she started off along the front of the house.

"Where are you going?"

"Maybe she's outside somewhere. Let's check it out…"

Sarah hurried to catch up with her cousin. Around the back of the house, she could see the ocean off to her right. The dunes were high, topped with beach-grass that swayed in the occasional gust of wind. Between two of the dunes, Sarah saw a wooden walkway.

"I don't see her back here," Emma said, focused on the back of the house.

When Sarah reached the gap between the dunes, she saw that the wooden walkway led out to the pier. It was a private entrance, which Sarah then realized must've been owned and controlled by the Jacobs family.

Her eyes ran along the wooden pier, the blissful scene marred by the yellow crime scene tape near the middle of the pier. Before the crime tape, she saw a figure.

"Emma," Sarah called over her shoulder. "Maybe that's her…"

"Only one way to find out," Emma said, rushing down toward where Sarah stood.

They walked out onto the pier, stepping closer to whoever was standing out there. Sarah's heart raced as they approached the mysterious person.

"Looks like a woman," Sarah said, now getting a

better look at the features that had been difficult to see with the glare of the sun.

As they grew closer, the woman turned around. She appeared to be in her late forties, maybe fifties. Her hair was up in a French twist, and she wore dangling earrings and a long, wispy dress that danced gently with the wind.

"This is a private pier," the woman called.

"Mrs. Jacobs?" Sarah asked.

The middle-aged woman stepped closer toward the entrance of the pier, where Sarah and Emma currently were.

"Who are you?" the woman asked, face scrunched up in a scowl.

"I'm Sarah Shores and this is my cousin, Emma. Larry Shores is our grandpa."

The woman stepped up so she was only a few yards from them, and she shaded her face with her hand, squinting. Suddenly, the sides of her mouth turned up slightly and her brows went from furrowed to relaxed.

"Oh, of course!" Charlotte Jacobs said. "How's Larry doing?"

Sarah and Emma approached her. "Good. He's staying busy at the boutique," Emma said.

"Ah yes, the pet boutique." Charlotte took a deep breath, shifting her gaze off toward the ocean. "I haven't been there in a while," she said, looking off into the water.

Sarah saw a couple walking down on the beach below. They disappeared under the pier for a moment, then reappeared on the other side and continued along.

"More and more tourists will be coming soon," Charlotte said, gazing upon the couple.

Sarah thought she saw a forlorn look in the woman's eyes. Perhaps she was thinking about her late husband.

Sarah said, "So sorry to hear about Mr. Jacobs."

Charlotte peered at the couple for a few long moments, then turned back to Sarah. "Thank you."

Emma said, "It's terrible."

"At least John lived a long, productive life," Charlotte said, as if she were trying to comfort Sarah and Emma. "It's unfortunate, sure, but he's had his fair share of time on this Earth."

"Are you okay?" Sarah asked.

"Yes. I'm fine."

"We haven't seen you around town much," Emma said.

The woman smiled. "Then you're not looking hard enough. I go into town to meet with my friends quite often."

"We ran into one of them today," Sarah said.

"Oh yeah?"

"Yeah. Marigold Dunham."

"Oh, of course. She's a sweetheart. Like a daughter to me."

Sarah nodded, choosing her next words carefully. Before she could say anything, Emma pulled out the picture of Marigold and her late husband.

"We were going through an old scrapbook and found this picture," Emma said, handing the picture to Charlotte.

"Well, look at that," Charlotte said, looking at the picture with a smile. It wasn't the reaction Sarah or Emma expected. "I remember that day well."

"You do?"

"Sure do. I took this picture."

Sarah looked at Emma for a moment, as Mrs. Jacobs stared at the picture, clearly filled with nostalgia.

"You took this picture?" Emma asked.

"Of course!"

"So do you get together with Marigold often?" Sarah asked.

"Yes," Charlotte said. "Just saw her last Friday. I was going to go to a dinner party, but I had a bad evening and didn't feel like being around too many people. So, Marigold picked me up, and I went to her place to stay the night."

Sarah and Emma exchanged glances again. Friday

was the night of the murder. So, as long as she wasn't lying, her story seemed to corroborate with Marigold's. Still, Sarah had to dig some more.

"Was that the night of—"

"Yes, imagine coming home to that news. But thank goodness for Marigold…"

"What do you mean?"

"Marigold had been helping me through a rough patch. John and I were in the middle of a divorce. That night, she was helping me cope with all the stress John was causing me. The whole legal battle and all. That evening, John was just downright miserable, angry. I'm lucky to have a friend like her who can keep such a big secret between us. I really didn't want the divorce to get out. You know how this town is with gossip."

"I'm so sorry to hear," Sarah said, keeping her face neutral.

Charlotte looked out at the waves crashing upon the shore and said, "All that mess gave me something to be tired about. But now…oh, I don't want to bother you with all of this."

Sarah smiled sweetly. "It's quite all right, Mrs. Jacobs."

"You can call me Charlotte," she said with a smile. "I just don't know how to feel right now."

"Maybe we should go. We shouldn't be bothering you during this time."

"Oh, it's fine. You want some lemonade or something?"

"Uh, no. We're alright," Emma said, politely.

Charlotte smiled. "How about some tea? I can make us some hors d'oeuvres and we can have ourselves a little tea party."

Emma and Sarah looked at each other for a moment before Sarah spoke. "No, we should be going. Grandpa is probably waiting for us."

Charlotte shrugged. "Suit yourself," she said, looking out toward the horizon.

Back at the boutique, Larry was finishing up helping a customer with the purchase of a collar and leash. He rang up the customer and bagged the items.

Sarah could tell he was in a good mood—the cash register was ringing.

Of course, the killer was still on the loose and she felt like they were farther away from figuring out who murdered John Jacobs.

"Okay, I'm going to get some dinner ready," Larry said.

Sarah nodded. "Sounds good."

"Hey, I have an idea! You can invite your friend Adam." Larry waggled his brows at Sarah.

"Will you stop that?" Sarah said. Her grandparents were always trying to set her up with Adam, ever since she was a kid.

Larry laughed.

Then it dawned on Sarah. Adam! She forgot to call him. She had been so wrapped up finding lead after lead that she'd forgotten to give him the update. Perhaps, with Adam there, they could go over what they knew and come up with a theory based on all of their current information.

"I'll text him," Sarah said.

"Now, that's the right attitude," Larry said. "Let him know I'll be making his favorite: lasagna with my super-secret sauce."

Sarah texted Adam, and received a message back accepting the invitation. A few seconds later, she received another text from Adam, stating he had something big to tell her about the Jacobs case and that he would tell her in person when he got there.

The hours passed, and the boutique had an intermittent flow of customers, mostly small-ticket items purchased by some locals.

With the shop empty of customers, Sarah and Emma

sat behind the counter. Rugby padded by, on his way to his water bowl. The sounds of him lapping up water filled the boutique.

The seconds ticked by as they sat in silence.

Emma said, "Was it just me or did Charlotte do a one-eighty back there?"

"I definitely noticed."

"Yeah, one minute she seems to be mourning her husband and the next she's smiling and ready to have a party."

"I wouldn't go as far as to say that, but her mood definitely changed."

"Almost like it was all an act." Emma paused. "And she seems to still be under the impression that it was an accident."

Sarah did pick up on Charlotte Jacobs calling her husband's death an accident, but chalked it up to the woman's grief.

"I don't know," Sarah said. "I mean, I guess we all grieve differently. And we have to take into consideration that they were in the middle of an ugly divorce."

"True."

Winston walked by, going over toward where Rugby now lay. The corgi yawned, which in turn caused Sarah to yawn.

"Yawns are contagious, even between species?" Emma asked.

"Apparently."

"So, I'm stumped."

"About what?"

"If Marigold and Charlotte were together the night of the murder, then who killed Mr. Jacobs?"

Sarah shrugged. "That's the million-dollar question. Let's see what Adam has when he gets here."

Before long, it was closing time. They locked up the store and took the dogs upstairs. Misty was already in the apartment, and fled upon seeing Rugby and Winston. Apparently, she wasn't in the mood to harass them.

Sarah saw that the table was set for four and smiled. It had been several years since she'd had dinner with Adam. She remembered the last time, they had talked about Adam beginning his career. She'd been impressed with his drive, and intrigued by his mission in life: to serve and protect, bringing justice to the small town of Cascade Cove.

Tonight's conversation, she knew, would be just as interesting.

A rap at the door caused both dogs to bark as they raced across the living room to greet their guest.

Larry answered the door.

"Hello there, Adam," Larry said, shaking the young man's hand.

"Hi, Mr. Shores."

Adam waved to Sarah and Emma, and they walked over to him, taking turns giving him brief hugs.

"You hungry?" Larry asked, putting his oven mitts on to check his masterpiece, sizzling in the oven.

"Famished."

"Long day?"

"Long *week*."

They all sat down around the dinner table. Larry asked, "Anyone want some wine? Got a few bottles of my favorites from Dunham Vineyards."

They agreed on a wine and Larry poured four glasses.

Larry lifted his glass and everyone else followed suit. "To a happy and prosperous peak season," Larry said, and they all clinked their glasses together.

"That's if the murderer is apprehended," Emma said.

Sarah noted her grandpa's expression sour slightly, but then he perked back up again upon taking a sip of the wine. "My favorite."

Adam sipped the wine as well and said, "I've never had Dunham's wine. It's delicious."

"Eh," Emma said, "I've had better."

Larry waved dismissively. "You don't know what you're talking about. Okay, now...Dig in, everyone."

They took turns filling their plates with a slice of Grandpa Larry's famous lasagna, salad, and homemade bread sticks.

"So," Adam said, setting his wine glass down after taking another sip. "I've found out something very interesting."

"What?" Sarah asked.

"I did some digging about what you told me earlier."

Emma leaned forward. "And?"

"It's about John and Charlotte..."

"Oh, I've been meaning to call Charlotte," Larry said.

"Grandpa," Emma said, "let Adam finish."

"Sorry."

Sarah took a sip of wine, waiting for Adam to continue.

"So," Adam said, "it turns out that a week before Mr. Jacobs passed, his life insurance policy was increased dramatically."

Sarah nearly spit her wine. She looked over to Emma and said, "My goodness. This changes everything."

CHAPTER 17

"It sure does," Adam said, taking a bite of his lasagna.

"They're probably both in cahoots," Emma said, shaking her head. "We learned that Marigold's car was parked outside Jacobs' house the night of the murder."

"We already knew about that," Adam said. "Charlotte was the first person we questioned about her husband's murder and she said that Marigold picked her up. She stayed the night with her. We then called Marigold in to corroborate her whereabouts."

Emma and Sarah looked at each other. "Why didn't you tell me that before?" Sarah asked.

"Didn't think it was important, I guess. Their stories matched on day one, so we ruled Charlotte out."

"Yeah, well after what you just found out about the life insurance policy being increased, they might very well be using each other as a means to a solid alibi."

"We still don't have any proof," Adam said.

"I know, but hear me out. Charlotte could've been growing tired of the cranky old man, and so she decides to get a divorce. That could net her half of his money."

"Unless he had her sign a prenup," Emma said.

"Prenups aren't common amongst us older folks," Larry chimed in.

"So why wouldn't she be happy with half of his wealth?" Adam asked.

Sarah scratched her chin. "Maybe Charlotte had asked Marigold for help with something regarding the divorce."

"Saw dollar signs," Emma said. "Probably put Charlotte up to getting Jacobs to increase the life insurance."

"Yeah," Sarah continued, "and if Charlotte didn't like her husband, it's not a stretch to imagine Marigold manipulating her into having her husband 'taken care of.'"

Emma nodded. "Right. It could be a whole 'out of sight, out of mind' deal, where Marigold took care of the deed in exchange for a cut of the money."

"Could also explain Charlotte's peculiar behavior back at the pier today."

"And Marigold dodging questions."

Adam looked at both Sarah and Emma. "What do you mean?"

Sarah and Emma told Adam about their run-ins with Marigold and Charlotte that day.

Adam took a sip of wine, then placed his glass down, clinking slightly against his plate. "Still pure speculation."

"I think it is," Larry said, wiping his face with a napkin. "Sarah, I think Emma's gotten into your head a bit, don't you think? Marigold is a sweet young lady and Charlotte is a kind woman. I don't see them causing harm to anyone."

Adam sighed, but remained silent.

Sarah said, "If the motive is money, which would definitely be the case for Marigold since she'll probably be losing the winery, then—"

"But why would Charlotte risk it?" Larry interrupted. "Maybe I can see the case for Marigold, I really can, but Charlotte...she's been around for quite a while and I don't think I've ever heard her hurt so much as a fly. I just don't see it."

"Instead of getting half through a divorce," Emma said, "she would get all of his fortune, plus the life insurance money. So even if Marigold got half, which would be more than enough, Charlotte would still come out way ahead."

Larry shook his head. "I just don't buy it."

"Well, it is *possible*," Adam said. "Marigold certainly has the motive: money. And Charlotte could have two possible motives: money and getting even with Jacobs. Divorce can be a nasty business."

"And they both have the opportunity to do it," Sarah said. "Don't have rock-solid alibis."

"Yeah," Emma said, "and they have the means. A blunt object would be all that's required to get the job done."

Sarah's face scrunched up. "Do you think either of them could drag the body to the pier, though?"

"You're saying they did it together?"

"Not necessarily. Charlotte could have agreed to allow it to happen, but Marigold could have had help…"

"Okay," Adam said, holding up his hand. "Let's not get too far ahead of ourselves. I'll muster up a case from what we know and run it by my colleagues, see what they have to say. Then in a day or two, I'll take both of them down to the station for questioning. From there, we'll see if we can get some answers and get to the bottom of this. Sound good?"

Both Sarah and Emma nodded.

"So, Adam," Larry said, "did you ever get any leads into who broke into my shop?"

"Not yet. We're still looking into that. But I'll keep you posted."

The next day, Sarah reorganized her knitted dog sweaters, adding more to the collection for the shop, as Emma was working on her laptop at the counter. Sarah felt proud of her latest creations. She'd learned a new stitch that she was able to incorporate into the sweater's design—an intricate type of Celtic cable stitch that ran down the back of the sweater. She was just folding the last sweater, adding it to the shelf, when Adam walked in.

"Another nice day," Adam said to Sarah.

"Hi, Adam," Sarah said, looking up to see Adam in his uniform. "They have you off desk duty now?"

"No, I'm on break. I was wondering if you wanted to go get some air?"

Rugby rushed over to greet Adam, who rubbed the yellow lab's head with both hands, causing the dog to pound his tail firmly on the floor in excitement. Winston trotted over and sat, waiting patiently for his turn. Adam laughed and then looked over at Emma.

"Hey, Emma," he said.

Emma was still in deep concentration and let out a grunt that kind of resembled a "hey" in response to Adam's greeting.

Sarah walked up to Adam. "She's still working on the website for the boutique."

"I thought she finished it," Adam said. He was trying to pet Winston, but Rugby kept pawing at his arm for more attention.

"Yeah, but Larry couldn't get into the admin section to add stock listings, and there was also an issue with the payment processing or something."

Adam shook his head. "Sounds like fun."

Sarah laughed. "But if you don't mind some extra company…" she said, motioning to Rugby and Winston.

"Sure, the more the merrier."

Sarah went to go grab the dogs' leashes, and said to Emma, "Do you mind?"

Emma looked at Adam. "Just as long as you don't have any more tips on the mystery of John Jacobs."

Adam shook his head. "Not yet."

Emma shrugged. "Then no, I need to finish this website, anyway. And I need to start putting that last order into inventory."

"Oh, you finally got that order?" Sarah asked.

"Yeah, came this morning."

"Good. Well, have fun, Emma."

"I'll try," Emma said, turning her attention back to her computer.

Sarah got the dogs leashed up and she and Adam strolled out the door that lead to the boardwalk.

Once outside, they turned right and walked along the boardwalk, taking in the sights and sounds. The sounds of people chatting were truncated by the occasional crashing of waves off to their left. Sarah picked up on the sweet smell of baked goods. A couple rollerbladed past them, waving as they went. The weekend was quickly approaching, though the abundance of new faces wasn't apparent to Sarah.

"I hope this season isn't a bust," Sarah said to Adam.

"It should be as good as last year, don't you think?"

"With an unsolved murder case? A killer on the loose?"

"Yeah, well, that could put a damper on things."

After a while, they turned right and strode down a walkway that acted as an access point, leading to the main road. Across the street, they reached the Banana Hammock Bar and Grill. There, Sarah spotted two women walking out into the parking lot.

"Is that Marigold?" Sarah asked, squinting.

"Looks like it," Adam said. "And look who she's with."

"Charlotte."

Adam started to walk across the street toward the women. Sarah followed him, hoping they could get some answers.

They crossed the street, Rugby and Winston next to Sarah.

"Hey, Charlotte!" Sarah called out, waving.

The beautiful, middle-aged woman waved back. "Hi, Sarah."

Marigold said hello to Adam, but didn't even look at Sarah. It was obvious she was still miffed about their altercation in that same parking lot the other day.

"Nice day to take the pups for a walk," Charlotte said.

Sarah felt Rugby tug on the leash as he tried to say his hellos to the women. "I'll say."

"I've been looking into your husband's case," Adam said, getting right to the point.

"Thank you for your help, officer," Charlotte said. "Have you found anything out about what happened with his murder?"

Sarah did a double-take. Last they talked to Charlotte, she was under the impression it was an accident, and neither Emma nor Sarah had corrected her in their attempt to get more information without inadvertently accusing the widow. Perhaps Marigold had mentioned that there was foul play involved, though the debutante had been put off by the very mention that anything other than accidental drowning was suspected.

The only explanation Sarah could think of was that Charlotte had slipped-up.

Sarah saw Marigold looking away, her gaze vacant. Sarah wondered what was on the woman's mind.

"Didn't you think he drowned?" Sarah asked Charlotte. "Accidental drowning…"

Charlotte sputtered, "I…uh…"

Marigold said, "She's been through enough. Now, if you don't mind, I'd like to take her back home so she can get her rest."

"Very quick," Adam said, "if you don't mind, Mrs. Jacobs…"

Marigold protested, but Charlotte waved her off like a pestering fly. "Go ahead, officer," Charlotte said.

"Could you tell me about Mr. Jacobs' life insurance policy? It appears to have been raised significantly a week before his death."

Before Charlotte could speak, Marigold said, "That's absurd! How dare you even bring that up at a time like this…Come on, Charlotte, let's go."

Marigold opened the passenger door to her yellow Beetle and hurried Charlotte in. She scowled at Sarah on her way around to the driver's side, started the engine, and sped off.

Sarah and Adam looked at each other.

Sarah said, "How much do you want to bet she'll be calling her lawyer when she gets home?"

Adam nodded. "Who knows…She might even be calling them as we speak."

CHAPTER 18

*B*ack at the boutique, Adam said his goodbyes and Sarah filled Emma in on what had transpired outside the Bar and Grill.

Emma chuckled. "They are so busted."

"Seems like it," Sarah said. "Adam said he will take them both to the station to question each of them individually. See if their stories match."

"You'd think their stories would line up perfectly. They probably have this all planned out. Can't believe Charlotte's slip-up, though. Guess she's not the mastermind like Marigold is..."

"Guess not."

"Hopefully they can get a confession from one of them before then. My money's on Charlotte caving in first."

Sarah nodded.

"Did you say Adam is stopping by later?" Emma asked.

"Yeah. They're going to Jacobs Manor right now to find them, and he'll probably stop over after their questioning."

"Excellent," Emma said, reaching down to get the dogs each a biscuit. "Hopefully he'll bring some exciting news with him. Now that would be something to toast to! Wouldn't it be ironic toasting their capture with Dunham wine?"

Sarah laughed. "Only you would think of that!"

That evening, Sarah lay in her grandpa's recliner, flipping through another one of Grandma's old scrapbooks. Winston had managed to wedge himself next to her, silently sleeping, unlike Rugby, who was next to the chair on the floor, snoring away. She'd taken the dogs for another walk and they were conked out. Misty, however, was restless, playing on the floor.

Sarah stopped at the old black and white photo of Mr. Walter Greensmith and George Jacobs. She studied both men. Walter had a smirk on his face and George Jacobs looked proud. Though, both men had their chests puffed out and were wearing suits. Walter had his jacket opened and something was peeking out from it. Sarah leaned in to get a better look, squinting her eyes.

"Hey," Emma said, walking in with the latest mystery book she was reading. She plopped down on the couch. "Still looking at those old, dusty scrapbooks?" She lay down and opened her book, removing the book marker.

"Wow, you read fast," Sarah said, noticing that her cousin was already halfway through the book.

Suddenly, a knock came at the door and the once-sleeping dogs were now lunging across the living room.

Sarah closed the scrapbook and laid it down on the coffee table. "That must be Adam."

"Oh, you think he's done questioning Marigold and Charlotte already?" Emma said, closing her book.

"I don't know, but he said he'd stop by once he was done." Sarah opened the door and Adam stepped in. Rugby jumped up at him.

"Rugby, no jumping. You know the rules," Sarah said, grabbing his collar.

Adam smiled. "That's okay. The big lug is just happy to see me." Adam bent down and ruffled Rugby's ears as Winston trotted over to say "hi" too. "Hey there, buddy." Adam looked up at Sarah. "Still no leads on who this little guy's owner is?"

"No. Still nothing. Bizarre, right?"

Adam nodded.

"So?" Emma said, looking at Adam expectantly.

"So," Adam said back to her. "Marigold and Charlotte have a solid alibi."

"What?" Emma practically shouted. "Everyone seems to have a solid alibi around here, don't they?"

Adam shrugged. "What can I say? They were very cooperative. They were straightforward and answered all our questions."

Sarah felt confused. "We're back to square one, I guess."

"So, what was their alibi?" Emma asked, using her fingers to imitate quotations while saying "alibi."

"Apparently, Marigold's maid was there."

Emma gasped. "She has a maid?"

"Yeah, a live-in maid. So she was there all night. Said she could speak for the women drinking wine and eating chocolate and hor d'oeuvres until almost 3:00 a.m."

"Wow." Emma shook her head. "Isn't that the life?"

Sarah was deep in thought. She couldn't understand who did it. All signs pointed to Marigold and Charlotte. It had to be them. They had motive, opportunity—even a life insurance policy. "What if the maid is covering for them?"

"Doubt it," Adam said. "She didn't seem all that happy

to be cleaning up after them at three in the morning. She said she's usually done by 9:00 p.m. and retires to bed every evening, but she knew when Charlotte came over it was going to be a long night."

Sarah just couldn't wrap her head around it not being Marigold or Charlotte.

Just then Larry came into the room. "Hey, has anyone seen that necklace?"

"It's on the bookshelf, where you left it," Emma said, pointing to it. "I can't believe you're still wearing that thing."

"Ah! Thank you, Emma." Larry walked over to the necklace.

"Wait, Grandpa," Sarah said. "You've been wearing that necklace?"

Larry held up the necklace, wearing a proud look. "Yeah. You should see the looks I've gotten this past week wearing this bad boy. Even Bob seemed intrigued."

Emma cut in, "Grandpa, maybe you shouldn't be wearing it. What if it's worth money or something? We should get it appraised. Right, Sarah?"

Sarah didn't respond. She was distracted by the picture she was looking at of Walter and George. Their suits and the way their chests were puffed out and...

Sarah walked over to the scrapbook and flipped

through it quickly, pulling out the picture of Walter and George. "Grandpa, can I see that necklace?"

"Sure." Larry took it off and handed it to Sarah. "Should I not wear it?"

"Where's your magnifying glass?"

Larry walked over to his junk drawer. "It should be in here somewhere," he said, rummaging. "Ah, here it is." Larry pulled out his magnifying glass and handed it to Sarah.

Emma and Adam looked at each other, confused.

Sarah sat down with the picture on her lap. She narrowed her eyes as she hovered the magnifying glass over the picture, adjusting the distance until she could see the object peeking from Walter's jacket clearly. There, she could see the object in the picture bore the same marking as the pendant she held in her hand. She looked at the necklace, delicately feeling the grooves of the engraved tree on the pendant. "Oh, my."

Finally, Emma spoke up. "What is it?"

"You all need to see this."

They all huddled around Sarah and the picture.

"See this?" Sarah started. "This pendant around Walter's neck has the same intricate markings as the pendant. See? It's a tree."

Adam said, "Okay, well, then I guess we found the owner."

Larry looked at Adam. "That's Walter. He's been dead for over a decade."

"Well, isn't your handyman, Bob, his son?"

"Ah, yes! It should go to next of kin. Won't he be happy we found it!" Larry said with a smile.

"Hold on," Sarah said. "Emma, where's that picture of Marigold and John Jacobs."

"It's in my room. Give me a sec, I'll go grab it." Emma ran out of the room.

When she was gone, Adam looked at Sarah. "What's going on?" he asked.

"Hold that thought."

Emma came rushing back with the photo and handed it to Sarah. Sarah took the picture. "Just as I thought."

"What?" Adam and Emma said in unison. Larry looked over Sarah's shoulder to try to see what she was seeing.

Sarah handed Emma the magnifying glass and the picture of Marigold and John Jacobs. "See what's peeking out from John Jacobs' jacket?" The pendant was only partially visible, showing some of the roots at the bottom and a couple of leaves at the top.

Emma gasped. "It can't be." Her eyes were wide in disbelief. "How in the world did I miss that?"

"You mean, how did *we* miss it?"

"What?" Adam repeated.

Emma gave him the picture and the magnifying glass. Adam took a look. Larry now leaned over Adam's shoulder, straining to see.

Adam looked up from the picture. "I don't get it."

"Don't you see?" Sarah began. "In the picture of Walter and George, Walter Greensmith is wearing the necklace. And in this picture, taken decades later, John Jacobs is wearing the necklace. How come Jacobs is wearing Bob's father's necklace?"

"That's intriguing, but it doesn't really mean anything."

Sarah shook her head. "No, it wouldn't. But add in the fact that Winston gave me this necklace when I found him. And Orloff, who was walking past the Jacob's house during the night of the murder, said he saw a small dog almost identical to Winston, coming from behind the Jacobs place."

"I don't know, Sarah. Just sounds like we found the rightful owner of the necklace, is all."

"Or we just found a motive," Emma said.

Adam shook his head. "I think you've been reading too many of your mystery stories."

"If that's your take away," Sarah said, "then I assume you don't know the history of these two families."

Adam looked at Sarah and then at Emma. "Okay. Fine, I'll bite."

Sarah turned to Larry. "Grandpa...you told me Walter Greensmith and George Jacobs were partners in a firm..."

Larry nodded. "Yeah. So?"

"You said they owned a lot of land back then. What happened?"

"All I know is there was a falling out between Walter and George, and John Jacobs got everything."

"How come you didn't bring this up earlier?"

"It happened a long time ago. Ancient history."

"So, what's the significance of the necklace?"

Emma said, "This necklace is an antique. Probably worth a lot of money or something."

Larry leaned in. "Can I see the necklace?" He stepped forward as Adam reached out to hand it to him.

Just then, a chipmunk rustled at the window sill. Rugby lunged across the living room to the window. In his haste, Rugby knocked into Larry, barking at the little critter, who scurried away quickly.

Sarah watched as the necklace flung into the air and slammed against the coffee table. The pendant split in half, and Larry cried, "Rugby, look what you made me do!"

Sarah and Emma's mouths dropped as they eyed the glinting piece of metal that now lay on the carpet.

Adam stepped closer to see the small, shiny item that had fallen from the pendant.

"What is that?" Emma asked.

Larry bent down and picked it up. "Looks like a small key."

Adam approached Larry, who picked up the key and was now holding it out to get a better look. "Looks like a key to a safe deposit box."

"Like at a bank?" Sarah asked.

"Probably."

Emma crossed her arms and grinned, proudly. "Sounds like motive to me."

Sarah shared the same smile. "There's only one way to find out. I think I have an idea."

CHAPTER 19

"I can't believe you talked me into this," Adam said, resting his elbow on the window of his car and propping his head up. They were parked down the street from the boutique in Adam's Honda, staking out the front of the shop during their impromptu "sting" operation. Adam was off duty but had some equipment from the station in his possession, which he reluctantly allowed them to use for this undertaking.

There was movement in the front window of the boutique, and Sarah could see her grandfather fidgeting and adjusting items on the shelves.

Sarah lowered her binoculars. "You want to be taken seriously at the station, don't you? And maybe get off desk duty."

"Yeah, but if you're wrong, I could lose my job."

"Trust me."

"I'm trying."

"You might even get a promotion!"

Adam groaned.

Sarah raised the binoculars back up to her eyes. "I think I see him."

Sarah grabbed her radio and held down the push-to-talk button. "Hey Grandpa, he's coming. Remember to show him the necklace and then place it somewhere visible."

Static emitted from the radio. "Maybe Emma should do this." Emma was hiding in the office, taking care of the dogs so that they weren't a distraction—and because she wanted to be nearby, in case Grandpa got into any trouble.

"No, Grandpa. He trusts you. He barely speaks to Emma. Just stick to the plan and it'll be fine."

"Okay, but just for the record: I don't like lying."

Sarah sighed. "Technically, Grandpa, you're not lying. Now turn off your radio."

Larry shut off the radio. It was understood that now Sarah and Adam would be able to hear what was going on in the boutique through the monitor on Adam's phone, which he attached to his dashboard. And if Larry needed help, he would use the code word they'd come up with.

Several moments later, Sarah and Adam could hear the chimes of the door open to the boutique on the phone screen. Her grandfather spent hours adjusting the hidden camera so they could get a clear angle. Adam told him he would do it since it's the station's equipment, but Larry was stubborn and said he could do it. Sarah had to admit, he got a perfect shot.

"Hi, Bob," Larry said.

On the camera, Bob came into view. She saw his flannel shirt and overalls. He walked briskly up to the counter. Adam and Sarah leaned toward the small monitor on Adam's dashboard to hear the conversation between Larry and Bob.

"Hey, Larry. So, you say you need me to take a look at one of your lights again?"

Sarah was proud of Emma for thinking of that one. Grandpa always needed those spotlights fixed.

"Yes, I need my light fixed. Can you help me?"

Bob chuckled. "That's why I'm here."

"Thank you. I will now take you to my light," Larry said almost directly into the camera.

"Say, Larry…Are you okay?" Bob asked.

"Why, yes, Bob. I am."

Adam looked like he was in pain. "He isn't a very good liar."

Sarah shook her head. "Maybe he's just nervous. I've

seen him lie before one time when Grandma got her hair done. It wasn't pretty."

Larry led Bob to the "broken" light and they chatted a bit. Larry seemed a lot more relaxed, and it didn't take Bob long to resolve the issue.

"There," Bob's booming voice emitted through the small monitor's speakers. "Simple fix."

"Thanks for coming out," Larry said. He stepped over to the counter and Sarah could see Bob staring intently as her grandpa took off the necklace and hung it behind the counter.

Larry continued, "So we're heading out of town tonight."

"That's nice," Bob said, staring at the necklace.

Sarah looked at Adam. "Looks like he's really eyeing up that necklace."

Adam nodded, not tearing his eyes from the monitor.

Larry continued, "Yeah, the girls want to take me out somewhere nice overnight. But they won't tell me where. Can you believe that? Say they want to treat me for being the world's best grandpa," Larry said.

Adam looked at Sarah. "Looks like Larry's getting better at lying."

"What are you saying?" Sarah gave Adam a nudge on the shoulder. "He *is* the best grandpa."

Adam laughed. "That's not what I meant."

Adam and Sarah both focused their attention back on the screen.

"Sounds fun." Bob's voice was monotone.

Sarah saw her grandpa smile at Bob. "Well, I've got to get packed up. Thanks again for coming out on such short notice."

Once Bob was gone, Larry looked into the camera. "Okay, the bait has been set. Now we wait…"

CHAPTER 20

Sarah sat in the passenger seat with Adam by her side. The sun had set a little more than an hour ago, and she was growing restless waiting for the suspect to pick up the bait they had planted. Still parked down the street, their eyes were both fixed on the boutique's front door. Larry and Emma were no doubt up in the apartment, glued to Emma's phone to monitor the necklace via the hidden surveillance camera.

Sarah looked up and saw that the apartment was cloaked in complete darkness. In fact, every light in the entire building was out, and it was only by the glow of the crescent moon that Sarah could see the front door to the boutique.

Larry had left the store's entrance unlocked, since he didn't want to deal with the aftermath of an actual break-in. Sarah figured it would be fine—it was common knowledge around town that her grandpa was often forgetful.

Now, all Sarah could do was wait.

After fifteen minutes, Adam said, "It's almost ten o'clock."

"Yeah?"

"And there's still no one."

"Give it time. Could be any minute now. You saw how he was looking at that necklace."

Adam nodded.

They waited in silence for a few more minutes, then Adam cleared his throat.

"So, how's city life?" he asked. "Do you like it?"

Sarah looked over at Adam. "It's a bit more hectic than the Cove."

Adam stifled a laugh.

"What?"

"Cascade Cove is a bit more hectic now, don't you think?"

Sarah nodded. "Hopefully me coming into town wasn't a bad omen."

Adam scoffed. "Oh please. You coming here was just what this town needed. Besides, I missed you."

"I remember the first time we met," she said.

Adam broke out into a fit of laughter. The boy he'd

been re-emerged, if only for just a moment. "Oh, wow. Meeting you was painful."

It was Sarah's turn to laugh. "I was busy trying to get that silly kite up in the air."

"Admit it: You weren't looking at where you were going—you plowed right into me. I'll never forget that. Then when I saw you, I was like, 'who in the world is this girl?'"

"That was the first summer my parents brought me to visit my grandparents. They'd only been down here a few years by that point. The pet boutique was on its first or second year."

Adam gazed into Sarah's eyes, still smiling. "Who would have thought that collision would spark a friendship that's lasted to this day."

Out of the corner of Sarah's eye, movement.

"Look," she said.

A man in a black hoodie meandered past the Bait and Tackle shop and stopped when he reached Larry's Pawfect Boutique. He turned and studied the main door, then looked around to ensure no one else was around.

Sarah and Adam both slinked down in their seats—it was too dark to be spotted, Sarah knew, but they wanted to be certain.

She watched as the man stepped up to the door.

"I can't believe it. You were right," Adam said.

The man checked the door, and it immediately swung outward. He looked around again, as if in doubt of whether or not he should go in.

"Go on," Sarah said. "Take the bait…"

Moments passed by at a snail's pace, and then the hooded man entered the boutique.

"Bingo," Adam said.

Sarah studied the phone on the dash, seeing the faint glow of the "emergency exit" sign illuminate the space behind the counter.

"There he is," she said, seeing the shadow sweep across the screen and rush behind the counter.

In less than thirty seconds, the hooded man was back outside the store, the locket dangling from his hand. He pocketed the locket, and rushed along the street, heading toward a parked car. The man opened the car door, and in moments, the car pulled out into the street.

Adam started his engine and pulled out, keeping his headlights off as he followed the car. The glow of a few street lights was sufficient enough to light their way.

The car turned down another road. "We'll just follow his taillights and see where they take us," Adam said.

Eventually, Adam had to turn on his headlights as they drove farther and farther inland, away from Cascade Cove. He stayed far enough back as to not raise suspicions, but not so far back that he'd lose the person they were pursuing.

"Where's he going?" Sarah asked, keeping her eyes on the car off in the distance, a single beacon in the darkness.

"He's turning," Adam said, and quickly sped up.

They followed him down another road, then another.

One turn after another, they kept far back but still had a visual of the distant taillights. Then, Sarah saw the bright red brake lights and in the next moment, the car was out of sight.

"Where did he go?" Sarah asked.

Adam slammed both hands on his steering wheel. "I can't believe it. We lost him!"

Up ahead, Sarah saw complete darkness.

Her heart sank.

This "sting" was a bust.

Now, she was certain, they'd never catch the killer.

Justice wouldn't be served, and peak season would arrive with a noted lack of vacationers and tourists. Her grandpa's boutique would finally go under and—

"Look," Adam said, his voice interrupting Sarah's thoughts. "Walter Drive."

Sarah looked at the street sign, her gaze shifting

down the tree-lined dirt road that seemed to lead into the abyss.

Adam stopped the car, putting it in Park.

"What are you doing?"

"Wait here."

Before Sarah could protest, Adam got out of the car, a flashlight in hand.

Sarah put down her window.

"Adam?" she said in a sharp whisper.

The cool wind slapped her in the face as she watched Adam hunch down. He was looking at something on the ground.

Adam rose in a hurry and rushed back into the car.

"I see fresh tracks in the mud," he said. "Plus, I think I know this road…"

"Walter Drive…You think…"

"I don't know," he said. "But I've patrolled out here a few times and there's a cabin at the end of this road."

Adam put the car back into Drive and turned down the road, extinguishing his headlights, leaving nothing more than the hazard lights to illuminate the path to the cabin.

"Okay, here we are," Adam said, parking. "Stay here."

"Are you kidding?" Sarah said. "No way. I'm going with you."

"No, you need to stay here. It could be dangerous. Lock the doors."

Sarah huffed and locked the doors.

Adam nodded. "I'll be right back."

Adam rushed along toward the cabin. A moment after that, he disappeared into the darkness.

Sarah sat in the car, alert. All she could hear were the crickets chirping all around her, but nothing else.

All of a sudden, she heard a bang.

Sarah scrambled out of the car, shutting the door lightly just as Adam had when he got out. She hurried along the same path Adam had taken moments before.

Sarah could see the car they had been following, headlights still shining, but she didn't see anyone around.

Her heart raced as she hunched over and ran. When she came to a big tree trunk, it was pitch black and she could barely see a thing.

Before she knew it, she felt someone grab her from behind and cover her mouth before she could scream.

Then she heard the person shushing in her ear. "I told you to stay in the car." Adam let go of Sarah and she turned around to face him.

"I heard something, and I thought you might be in trouble."

Adam sighed. "I heard it too. I think it was the car. It backfired or something."

Just then, Sarah heard a car door close.

Adam put his finger up to his lips and looked around the tree trunk. He turned back to Sarah and said, "Someone's getting out of the car."

Sarah peeked around the other side of the trunk and saw the man who'd exited the vehicle, stepping in front of the headlights for a moment. His hood was now down, but she still couldn't see his face.

He pulled the necklace from his pocket, letting it dangle from his hand.

A sound off in the distance, probably a wild animal or something, startled the man, and he turned around to investigate.

The headlights illuminated the man's face and Sarah gasped.

Adam's voice came out in a whisper. "Is that…"

Sarah's eyes were as big as saucers as she tried to comprehend what she was seeing.

Time seemed to stand still as she stared at the familiar face. She couldn't believe it when her mind finally came to grips with the actual identity of the man.

CHAPTER 21

Sarah's mind flashed an image of the first time she saw the young man who now stood before them. The man who had apparently "turned a new leaf."

No, it couldn't be...

"Danny?" Adam whispered, peering out to get a good look at the man who gazed out into the darkness, practically blinded by his headlights. "Doesn't he work at Patricia's Tea Room now?"

"Yeah, he's Patricia's grandson...Bob's kid."

Danny turned and walked toward the entrance to the cabin.

"Look," Sarah said, pointing to the side of the cabin. "There's an open window. Maybe we can see in..."

Adam nodded, then they raced from the cover of the

tree toward the cabin. Hopefully Danny wouldn't come back out, or else they'd surely be spotted.

After a dozen tense seconds, they were alongside the house, crouched below the open window. Light peered out, illuminating the ground beyond the cabin. They, however, were still in the shadows. Safe, for now.

"I got it," came Danny's voice.

So, he wasn't alone.

Another voice boomed. "Second try's a charm. Hand it over, Danny."

Sarah wondered what he meant by that. Then it dawned on her—the break-in at her grandpa's shop.

Sarah was tempted to look into the window, but she wasn't sure if she'd be able to do so without being spotted.

She heard the sound of the locket being opened, then Danny said, "The old man mustn't have known what he had—there's still a key in there."

"Thank goodness," the booming voice said. "Okay, help me pull back the rug. The safe is under here."

"Do we have to go down in the basement?"

"There is no basement. The opening to the safe is facing upward, under the trap door."

"How did you find out about it, anyway?"

"I did some digging."

Sarah thought the booming voice sounded familiar.

Where had she heard that voice before? She was about to speak when she saw Adam press his index finger vertically against his lips.

Time seemed to slow as Sarah waited.

Crickets still chirped off in the woods.

Then Sarah heard the sound of a creaking hinge.

Boot steps.

A bang.

Then just woodland sounds again.

"It's not working," the booming voice said.

"Are you sure?" came Danny's reply, worry consuming every syllable.

"I know how a key works."

Silence.

"Nope, it's not the right key," the voice boomed.

"I bet that slug, Jacobs, switched it out before we offed him?"

Sarah's ears perked up and Adam pulled out his phone. He gave it a few taps with his thumb and slid it back into his pocket.

"I didn't 'off' him. It was an accident."

"Whatever you want to call it, old man. You killed him."

Sarah couldn't hold back much longer. She had been piecing it all together. The murder, the break-ins, the family history. She took the key from her pocket.

Adam looked at her. "What are you doing?" he whispered.

"It's time."

"No, it's time when I say it's time."

"Just cover me and follow my lead," Sarah said and went to the door of the cabin.

Adam grunted and followed her, probably knowing he didn't have a choice. When Sarah made up her mind, no one could stop her.

The front door was already open, and Sarah stopped just outside the doorway. "Is this what you're looking for?" Sarah held the key up into the beam of the moonlight as she stepped into the doorway. Adam was next to her, his gun aimed and ready.

Both men looked up at her. Danny spat, "You're on private property, you need a warrant to—"

"We heard everything," Adam said. "Two witnesses—one a cop—against you two...I don't think you'll have a chance."

"I didn't kill anyone. It was an accident!" Bob said, his face red and eyes somber. He looked like he was ready to weep.

"Dad, don't say anything to—"

"Don't you understand?" Bob began. "John Jacobs and his father. They stole from us. They took everything away from us."

Sarah lowered the key and looked at it. She considered what her grandpa had said about the falling out between the two families and the fact that John Jacobs had gotten everything. "Yeah," Sarah said. "George took your family's land, your wealth, and gave it to his son, John Jacobs." She held the key between her forefinger and thumb. "This key is what you were looking for when you broke into my grandfather's shop."

Bob's eyes welled up. "Your grandpa is a kind man. I would never do that to him."

"Yeah, but your son would."

Danny scoffed. "You have no proof."

"Oh, you'd like to think that, wouldn't you?" Sarah smiled. "But we have cameras. Who do you think planted that necklace? Luckily, my grandpa is a pack-rat and has a bunch of old safe deposit keys that have no use anymore, like the one in your hand right now."

Danny swallowed hard.

"And your Nana..." Sarah continued.

Danny glared at Sarah, looking like he was ready to strike at any moment.

Adam said to Sarah, "Okay, we should probably—"

But Sarah continued, "What John Jacobs did to your Nana that day was the last straw for you, wasn't it?"

Danny looked like he was ready to explode. "That wasn't me," he said with gritted teeth.

"Then who was it?"

"You wouldn't understand."

"Try me."

"My dad got angry that day, and he had every right to be. It was the last straw for him. After all the Jacobs family had done to our grandfather and to him and our family, then Jacobs raises the rent, trying to put my Nana out of business. But she's resilient, and so he comes barging into her Tea Room and puts on a show trying to put her business under. Doesn't pay her for the cookies she baked for him and gives her a heart attack. She almost died. And no one would have gone after Jacobs. They never do. He's too rich and powerful—with *our* money. I was the one who was at the hospital holding Nana's hand."

"Until your father called you."

"I'm glad my father finally did something. He went over there to confront him. He said they had a scuffle and Jacobs fell down the steps and he started freaking out. So he called me."

"And then you came over to finish the job."

"Like I said, he was freaking out. I told him he wasn't breathing and what's done is done. Told him to get the necklace and I'll take care of Old Man Jacobs. Wrapped him up and I drug him out onto the pier and dumped him. Tied some bricks to him to weigh him down."

"Apparently you're not very good at tying knots," Adam said.

"What can I say? I was never a great Boy Scout."

Sarah added, "And you forgot to consider the fact that John Jacobs is afraid of water. He doesn't even go out onto the pier. It's what tipped us off in the first place that this wasn't an accident."

Danny shrugged. "I didn't know."

Bob began crying. "I forgot. It slipped my mind that night with everything happening." Bob looked back at Sarah and Adam. "I swear, it was an accident."

"If it was an accident, then your son didn't have to dump his body like that."

Danny's face flushed red with anger. "Yes, I did. If I didn't, we would never get what's rightfully ours." Danny turned to Sarah and Adam. "It wasn't my fault. I had to do it."

In the background, Sarah could hear sirens growing louder. Brakes screeched outside and the sound of car doors slamming shut filled the air.

"I still don't understand..." Bob said, looking puzzled. "I looked all over for the necklace that night but couldn't find it anywhere. How on Earth did Larry get it?"

Sarah said, "It was a special delivery from our new friend, Winston. He must've been at the scene of the crime and scooped up the locket before you spotted him."

"Winston?" Then Bob's confused expression left his face as the realization struck him. Sarah knew he couldn't miss her bright green flyers all over town with the corgi's name in big, bold font on it.

"I take it you've seen my flyers."

The handyman nodded, face still sullen.

A couple officers rushed into the cabin, led by the town's sheriff, a stocky man with a graying beard that was neatly trimmed. In short order, the men slapped handcuffs on Bob Greensmith and his son, Danny. Both men were silent on their way out, hanging their heads in shame.

The sheriff said to Adam, "Looks like you won't be on desk duty as often, now that you cracked this case. Good work, Dunkin."

Adam shook the sheriff's hand and smiled. "I couldn't have done it without Sarah here."

The sheriff regarded Sarah and tipped his hat. "Thank you, ma'am."

"You're welcome," Sarah said, then she held the key out. "This is the key to the safe over there—they broke into my grandpa's boutique to get it."

The sheriff took the key from Sarah. "Let's have a look," he said. "See what all the fuss is about."

The sheriff stepped over to the open trapdoor and crouched down. The other men gathered around, including Sarah and Adam, to get a glimpse at whatever was inside. The sheriff slid the key into the lock and turned it slowly. An audible *click* emanated from the safe.

Sarah craned her neck to get a good view as the sheriff opened the safe. There were hundreds of gold coins stacked to one side, stacks of cash in the middle, and some papers to the right.

The sheriff turned toward Adam and Sarah. "Wow. At today's gold prices, there has to be close to a million dollars' worth in here."

"What are those papers?" Adam asked.

The sheriff leafed through them, and stopped abruptly when he realized what they were. "My goodness…these are deeds."

"To what?" Sarah asked.

"To many of the properties in Cascade Cove."

"Wow."

"I'd say at least fifty different properties—parcels of land, a dozen or so of the rental houses north of town, many of the businesses along the main strip, and of course, Jacobs Manor."

Sarah's jaw dropped slightly. It was clear to her that a lot was at stake in the dispute between the two families.

Not only a small fortune of gold and cash, but also what amounted to nearly a quarter of the properties in the small beachside town.

"That's crazy," Adam said, shifting his weight to one side.

"I'll say," the sheriff said, standing back up. He regarded Sarah, smiling. "If it weren't for you, those men would have made off with all of this. And they'd have gotten away with murder if it wasn't for you helping us."

"You're welcome."

"Too bad you're leaving next week," Adam said. "You'd be a good set of eyes and ears to have around town..."

"You don't live in the area?" the sheriff asked Sarah.

"No, sir," she said. "I'm staying with my Grandpa Larry while on vacation."

"Oh, of course. Larry," the sheriff said, chuckling. "Hopefully you stick around a while. Cascade Cove could use more upstanding citizens like yourself."

"We'll see," she said.

The sheriff shook her hand and then patted Adam on the shoulder. "Let's get this wrapped up and call it a night."

After giving her statement, Sarah was told she was free to go.

"I'm going to take her home," Adam said to the sher-iff. "I'll see you in the morning."

The sheriff waved to Sarah and Adam and they stepped out from the cabin. They walked out into the darkness toward his car, and for the first time in a few days, she truly felt safe. Once inside the Honda, he started it and pulled away from the cabin, then drove off along the desolate road.

"This'll be one for the books," Adam said.

"Yeah, wait till Larry and Emma hear about this," Sarah said. "And once my grandma catches wind, she'll probably clip the newspaper article out and put it in one of her scrapbooks. Part of the town lore."

"The town lore," Adam repeated, nodding. "What a way to start the season…"

CHAPTER 22

A few days later, Sarah was out with Rugby and Winston, taking them for a morning walk around town. She could see more and more shop owners preparing for the first week of the busy season. She couldn't believe she had been there over a week already, and so much had happened.

Passing by Fudderman's Bakery, Sarah waved when she saw Henry out front.

"Out to get some fresh air?" Sarah asked.

"Of course," Henry said. "Been working my tail off for tomorrow."

"Tomorrow?"

"Start of the peak season!"

"Oh yeah, of course. Well—"

"Hey, Sarah!"

Sarah turned and saw her cousin Emma across the street.

Turning back to Henry, she said, "I'll be over later for a Cruller."

"I'll be here!"

Sarah crossed the street and approached Emma.

"I still can't believe what you did last night," Emma said. "You're, like, a super hero crime fighter now."

Sarah laughed and then walked along, passing by Patricia's Tea Room.

Then Sarah saw Patricia Greensmith stepping out, her granddaughter Nancy by her side. They sat at one of the street-side tables, and Sarah and Emma approached them.

"Hi, Sarah. Emma," Patricia said. "Are you here for some tea?"

Sarah said, "Just out for a walk. I'm sorry—"

"Please, dear," Patricia said, taking a sip of her tea. "Don't be sorry. Danny can be a good boy, but he has a bad streak in him. Always has. In fact, we had to send him away to military school. Thought that would shape him up. I guess not." Patricia frowned. "Though, I am surprised that my son, Bob, got himself mixed up in all this. He was nothing like his father. My late husband, Walter, got himself into a bunch of shady deals."

"Shady deals?"

"Let's just say, George Jacobs was a master at getting what he wanted, and he got some dirt on Walter that he couldn't leave alone. Something about Walter embezzling money from a company he worked for, which wouldn't surprise me. Anyway, one thing led to another and Walter ended up making George Jacobs his sole beneficiary, if you can believe that. I guess to make sure he kept it hush-hush."

"Wow," Sarah said. "So—"

"So, when my husband passed away, everything went to George... and when he passed away, John Jacobs got everything. It didn't bother me that much—I had my tea shop and was content. Didn't want to go through all of the legal stuff, if you know what I mean. But Bob, on the other hand...it didn't bode well with him. He wasn't in the position to take any legal action, and I know it bothered him, but I didn't know it bothered him *that* much. Needless to say, he wasn't a fan of John Jacobs after he found out about all of that."

"I guess not."

There were a few moments of silence between them and then Emma asked, "So, are you okay?"

"Right as rain," Patricia said. "I have Nancy here— she's my rock."

Nancy smiled, sipping her tea. Apparently, she

shared her grandmother's view of her brother and father.

"I do what I have to," Nancy said. "Just glad to be here with Nana. We're all set for tomorrow."

Patricia smiled. "Oh, and Charlotte stopped by yesterday to see how I was doing. What a sweetheart."

"Really?" Sarah asked. "That was nice of her."

"Yeah, and everyone's talking about what she did."

Sarah glanced at Emma, who shrugged. "What did she do?" Sarah asked.

"She reversed John Jacobs' rent increase on all of his tenants. Can you believe it? She's an angel."

"Wow," Sarah said. "I bet they're all happy."

"That's an understatement. They were probably partying all weekend!"

Sarah and Emma laughed.

"Well, we better get back to help Grandpa," Sarah said. "He's been frantic about the busy season, making sure everything is in tip-top shape."

"Sounds good," Patricia said. "I'll see you two later."

Sarah and Emma said their goodbyes and walked the dogs back to the boutique.

Back at Larry's Pawfect Boutique, Sarah saw a police cruiser parked out front.

"I wonder what's going on," Emma said.

Inside, Sarah heard the bell jingle above her head.

She scanned the store and spotted Adam browsing along the far-left wall. He turned around and smiled when he saw her.

She let Rugby and Winston off their leashes, and they both rushed over to Adam.

Sarah watched as Emma walked toward the counter, and surveyed the rest of the store to see if she could find Larry.

"Where's my grandpa?" she asked Adam.

"In the back office on a phone call."

Adam pulled a couple treats from his pocket and handed one to each dog.

"Since when did you start carrying treats?" Sarah asked.

"Since I wanted every dog in town to absolutely adore me."

"So, what's up?"

Adam walked toward the middle of the shop where Sarah stood. Sarah saw her grandpa emerge from the back office to greet Adam.

"Just stopped by to let you know that the John Jacobs case is officially closed."

"I still can't believe my handyman did it," Larry exclaimed. "It's crazy, is what it is. Now, who am I going to call to fix things around this place?"

"I don't know. I guess there's a new job opening in

the Cove. Either way, I'm just glad this town can get back to normal."

"Thank goodness," Emma said. "But what are we going to do about excitement around here now?"

"Oh, there's some excitement that's coming our way," Larry said, a sly grin on his face.

"What?" Sarah asked.

Larry lifted his cell phone up in the air. "I was just on the phone with your grandma. She'll be back near the end of the week!"

"What happened to her job on the cruise ship?"

"She finished up with a shorter cruise, and then someone she works with needed extra work. She knew you were in town, Sarah, and so she pulled some strings, and voila!"

"Crazy Grandma," Emma muttered.

Sarah couldn't wait to see her grandma. It had been a long time since they were in Cascade Cove at the same time. Typically, when the planets aligned and she saw both her grandpa *and* her grandma, crazy shenanigans ensued. She was certain a whole load of fiascos was on the horizon.

"Well," Sarah said, smiling, "this will be interesting."

CHAPTER 23

That afternoon, the store was busier than it had been since Sarah arrived in Cascade Cove. More and more people were arriving by the hour, many of whom brought their pets. As per tradition by many of the regular vacationers, Larry's Pawfect Boutique was among their first stops.

The bell above the door jingled, and Sarah smiled. She and Emma were already working with one customer, and Larry was off to one side working with another.

Rugby and Winston were roaming about, saying hello to the customers and their dogs alike.

"Welcome! I'll be right with you folks," Larry said to the incoming customers, then walked over to the register with his current customers and rang them up.

"What about this leash?" the woman was asking Emma.

Sarah was about to ask the newest customers if they needed any assistance when her cell phone vibrated in her pocket. She pulled it from her pocket, expecting it to be Adam, but it was a number she didn't recognize. She let the call go to voicemail, then helped the customers.

"Hi there," she said, looking down at the beagle. "Oh, look…it's Sherlock!"

Val laughed. "You remember him?"

"How could I forget?"

"Where's Watson?" Phil asked.

Suddenly, the corgi rushed over to greet them. "*Winston,*" Sarah corrected.

"Did you ever find his rightful owner?" Val asked.

Sarah grimaced. "Not yet. Haven't got a single call about it. I put it in all the local papers and everything."

Val nodded. "Well, hopefully things work out."

"Thanks."

After ringing Val and Phil out, Sarah gave Sherlock a bone, and waved goodbye as they left the store. There was a lull in store traffic, so Sarah took the opportunity to check her phone. She saw that whoever had called her earlier had left a voicemail.

Emma cozied up next to her and bumped her in the side with her hip. "It's only going to get busier. The last couple I saw said they almost didn't come, but they heard about the murder case officially wrapped up, so they decided to come after all. You really did save the day."

Sarah nodded. "All in a day's work," she said, smiling.

Sarah lifted the phone to her ear, and listened to the message: "Hi, this is Zach over at the Cozy Beachside Rescue Center, in Filbertsville. We just saw your ad in the newspaper about the corgi, Winston. If you could please give me a call back…"

Sarah lowered the phone from her ear, her jaw dropping.

"What is it?" Emma asked.

Larry stepped over, intrigued. Winston was by his side.

Sarah stared down at the corgi and muttered, "It's about Winston."

"What?"

Sarah played the message on speaker phone for both of them to hear.

"Well, I'll be," Larry said. "He escaped from the Rescue, somehow, and travelled along the beach, past Jacobs Manor, and all the way here!"

"Yeah," Sarah said. She thought she'd be more excited that the mystery of the lost corgi had been solved, but as she stared down at Winston, she couldn't bear to see him go. "I...I'm going to miss him."

Larry nodded, crossing his arms. "Yeah, we're all going to miss him, but at least he'll get to go back to his rightful owners. We need to do what's best for him."

"I know," Sarah said, crouching down to pet Winston. "I guess I should call them and see what they have to say."

Rugby came over to her as well, and she gave both of them a bone.

With phone in hand, Sarah dialed the number back, and in two rings, heard the man's voice. "Hi, this is Zach."

"Hi, Zach. This is Sarah—I had the ad in the paper about the lost corgi, Winston."

"Of course," Zach said. "So glad you found him. We've been looking everywhere for him."

"I'm sure Winston will be glad to be reunited with his owners again."

Zach cleared his throat. "Well, he doesn't have any owners at the moment. We've been housing him, waiting for someone to adopt him and hopefully give him his forever home."

Sarah looked over at Larry, her eyes wide with excitement.

Into the phone, she said, "I...I was thinking I could adopt Winston."

"Have you adopted before?"

"Yeah, I have a yellow lab I adopted a few years ago, and he and Winston get along so well together. He's practically become part of the family here..."

"That's great! Of course, you'd have to come by with Winston so we can interview you and see if you and Winston are a good fit, and there's a bit of paperwork you'd have to fill out.

I'm sure you understand the process if you've adopted before."

"Of course," Sarah said. "When can I stop by?"

"How about tomorrow?" Zach asked. "Are you available?"

"Let me check," she said.

To Larry, she said, "Is it okay if I go tomorrow morning? I know it's the first day of busy—"

"No problem," Larry said, waving dismissively.

Sarah said into the phone, "I can stop by first thing tomorrow morning."

"Great," Zach said. "I'll see you then."

Sarah looked down at Winston, who was sitting at her feet, watching the bustle in the boutique. She thought about the first day she saw Winston. How he followed her, and how he quickly became a part of the family. He chose her. She reached down and pet his head.

"Welcome home, Winston."

The next day, Sarah rose early. She ate a bowl of cereal and got a shower, then once dressed, leashed up Rugby and Winston to get ready to head to the Cozy Beachside Rescue Center.

On her way toward the door, she saw Emma, who stretched groggily.

"Are you ready?" Sarah asked.

Emma nodded, and smiled. "Sure am. You said we'd make it back in time, right?"

"Yeah, Grandpa insisted that he'd be okay for the first hour or two running the boutique if we didn't make it back in time."

"Okay," Emma said. "Let's get a move-on."

In fifteen minutes, they were driving along in Sarah's Corolla, all the windows down. In the back, Rugby and Winston were enjoying the warm air cascading through the car.

"There's Jacobs Manor," Emma said as they drove past the hulking structure.

Sarah thought of the events that had passed and

sighed. What a week, she thought. But she had gotten to the bottom of the incident of John Jacobs and she hoped nothing bad like that ever happened again in the little town she enjoyed visiting every summer.

"So, you're only staying for one more week?" Emma asked.

"Yeah."

"It'll go by quick."

Sarah nodded as they made their way out of town, traveling along the two-lane road. Between dunes, she saw the ocean off to her right as they headed north. She thought about the fact that she'd be heading even farther north before she knew it. The summer would pass by quickly, and she'd be back at the school wishing for the next summer to come.

"Everything goes quick. Especially back in New York City."

"Things go at a snail's pace down here," Emma said. "Why do you think I stuck around? Get to work along-side grandpa and bring his business into the twenty-first century."

"You mean the website?"

"Yeah. The busy season is hectic, but once things calm down again and all the tourists leave, then the days will be long and we'll probably be able to get the online orders packed and shipped before lunch. Then I can relax on the beach and read a good whodunit mystery novel."

"Okay, now I'm getting jealous."

Emma laughed. "You know, you could just move down here?"

Sarah sighed, knowing what her cousin had suggested was a possibility. But still, she was scared.

Sarah furrowed her brow. Scared of what, though?

"I...I don't know. I mean, I doubt Grandpa needs anyone to—"

"Grandpa was actually talking to me a few days ago about how, if we have a great season, he's actually going to take my advice and use some of the money to start his own line of products."

"Really?"

"Yeah, really. And since you cracked the case just in time, I bet we'll have an excellent summer after all. Then, we'll need to hire another full-timer to help with the Larry's Brand rollout—he wants to sell his products in boutiques all over the country, and we'll need all hands on deck."

"Wow," Sarah said, raising her eyebrows.

"Yeah. Too bad you aren't staying longer to help..."

"I doubt Grandpa would want me to—"

"Are you kidding? He's been egging me on to ask you

to stick around. Said he couldn't bring himself to ask you himself…"

"I don't know what to say."

"You don't have to say anything. Picking up and moving is not something you should decide now, while driving," Emma said, laughing. "Just think about it, and let him know if you're interested. He knows you have a life up in New York, so no hard feelings…"

"Okay," Sarah said, seeing the signs for Filbertsville. "I'll let him know what I decide."

CHAPTER 24

*P*eak season began without a hitch, and business at Larry's Pawfect Boutique was better than they'd seen in years. Over the first week, Sarah noted many new and familiar faces alike. Those first few days were a litmus test for how the rest of the season would fare, and Sarah considered the initial days to be a success.

On the night before she'd planned to go back home to New York City, Sarah joined Adam, Emma, and Larry at the Banana Hammock Bar and Grill. Inside, she saw Kacey was overwhelmed.

"Good thing you got a reservation," Kacey said. "We're bursting at the seams here."

"And if history serves as any indicator," Larry said,

"I'll be bursting at the seams by the time I leave this place."

They were seated toward the center of the restaurant, and Sarah saw that nearly every table was full. Business was hopping everywhere now, and it would only get better.

The waitress came over, pep in her step. "Hi there, I'm Flo. What would you all like to drink?"

"Do you happen to have any Dunham Vineyards wine?" Larry asked.

"Of course," Flo said. She brought them a wine list and they made their selection. "I'll give you a few minutes to look over the menu."

Flo strode away, and Sarah looked down at her menu. She scanned the selections, unsure of what to get. She considered the Fish Tacos, a blackened catch of the day wrapped in a grilled flour tortilla. Her mouth watered as she read the rest of the description, which featured bacon, lettuce, and tomatoes. Of course, the meal was also served with their famous tortilla chips and home-made salsa.

She scanned down the page with her index finger, hearing her Grandpa's voice: "I'm thinking of getting the Banana Hammock Seafood Combo."

"You aren't going to try the Cascade BBQ Burger?" Adam asked. "That's my go-to at this place."

Sarah spotted the listing on the menu for the burger. "Oh my," she muttered. "Stacked with bacon, cheddar cheese, shredded lettuce, and the famous Banana Hammock BBQ sauce."

"Heard they bottle that stuff for people to buy," Emma said.

"They do," Adam said, grinning.

Flo brought the wine over to the table and, after uncorking the bottle and pouring each of them a glass, asked, "Are we ready to order any appetizers?"

"I think we're ready to order our meals," Larry said, getting the consensus from the table.

Everyone nodded, and Emma was the first to order.

"I'll take the Cascade Burger," she said.

Sarah looked at its listing on the menu. It had American cheese, lettuce, and tomato, and she was tempted to change her mind and copy off of Emma.

"And you, ma'am?" Flo asked.

"Uh," Sarah started. "I think I'll go with the Fish Tacos."

She figured she could try Emma's burger and perhaps get it another time.

Flo regarded Adam and said, "And your regular?"

"Yeah, BBQ Burger."

"And for you, sir?" Flo asked Larry.

"I'll have what he's having," Larry said, smiling.

"You won't regret it," Adam said with a chuckle.

Flo swept their menus off the table and sauntered away.

Larry then led the way in raising his glass and everyone else followed suit.

"To Sarah and Adam," Larry said, "for putting two baddies behind bars and bringing justice to Cascade Cove."

Then Larry looked over at Sarah and asked, "Want to toast anything?"

"To another wonderful busy season at Cascade Cove!"

They clinked their glasses together and everyone took a sip.

"Love this wine," Adam said, admiring the label on the bottle, which sat in the middle of the table.

"What do you think of this one?" Sarah asked Emma.

Emma nodded, then took another sip. "I...I kind of like this one."

"Really?" Larry asked. "I thought you weren't keen on Dunham wine!"

"I'm coming around to it."

Out of the corner of her eye, Sarah saw a familiar face. "Speaking of Dunham," she muttered.

Yes, it was Marigold Dunham, out with Charlotte again.

Marigold and Sarah exchanged glances, and then Marigold approached their table.

Marigold said her hellos and made small talk for a few moments. Looking at Sarah, she said, "I wanted to say how sorry I am about the other day, and how I lost my temper."

"No, Marigold. I'm sorry," Sarah said.

"Oh, please. I wasn't really cooperating—I was just trying to protect Charlotte. She's my best friend and has been through thick and thin with me."

"I understand. But I shouldn't have accused you of something as heinous as a murder like that."

"Honestly, now that I understand your side of it, I would have thought it was me too."

Charlotte approached the table and said, "Thank you again for capturing the men who did this to my husband."

Emma asked, "How are you holding up?"

"I'm doing fine. Better knowing that my husband's murderers are behind bars. Even though we were in the middle of a divorce, he still didn't deserve what happened to him."

Emma nodded, and Charlotte continued, "Interesting thing is, he wore that locket all the time—I never knew there was a key in it. He just told me that it was a family heirloom."

Before anyone could reply, the waitress came with their food.

"Well," Marigold said. "Charlotte and I should let you go."

"Oh, Charlotte," Sarah said. "I heard you brought the rent back down for your tenants."

"What John did was unnecessary—there was no reason for it," Charlotte said. "We have plenty of funds coming in. And besides, it's the least I could do—the people of Cascade Cove are like family to me. Anyway, enjoy your meals—got to love that they use all home-made ingredients here."

"Yeah, can't wait to dig in," Larry said, and the two women walked back to their table.

Over the next hour, they ate while talking about the weeks that had passed and the weeks to come.

After they finished and were waiting for the check, Sarah felt a tap at her foot under the table. She looked over at Emma and furrowed her brow.

Then a flash of realization struck her. It was time to break the news!

"Grandpa," Sarah said, "I have something I wanted to tell you."

"Oh yeah?"

"I've been thinking all week about my life back up north, and realized that my two weeks down here is the best part of my year. I heard you needed help rolling out your new brand of dog paraphernalia…"

Larry smiled and nodded, letting his granddaughter continue.

"…and if it's okay, I'd love to stick around for the rest of the summer and help out with the family business."

"Oh, Sarah," Larry started, and Sarah could see his eyes had reddened. He reached into his trousers' pocket for a handkerchief and dabbed his eyes with it. "That's the best news I've heard in a long time. Your grandma will be thrilled as well."

"Where is Grandma?" Emma asked.

Larry looked at his watch. "She should be getting in soon."

"Does she need someone to pick her up?" Adam asked. "I could run over and get her. Haven't seen Mrs. Shores in a long time."

"Thanks for the kind offer," Larry said, "but she's an independent woman—she has her own car parked at the port. She might even be back by the time we wrap up here."

"Can't wait to see her," Sarah said.

They paid the bill and left the restaurant, the sound of dozens of conversations melding into one with interspersed sounds of clinking glasses and silverware.

They strode back along the main strip, Larry and

Emma leading the way, with Sarah and Adam walking side-by-side behind them.

"So how was work this week?" Sarah asked.

"Things have definitely calmed down."

"Officially off desk duty?"

"Yeah," Adam said, "and you'll never believe this—Captain promoted me."

"Congratulations, Adam!"

Sarah gave Adam a hug, and it lasted a little longer than usual.

After their embrace, Adam said, "So the—"

Adam's cell phone rang suddenly, and he pulled it from his pocket.

"I have to take this," Adam said. "Even though I'm off duty now, I'm never *actually* off…"

Adam stopped, and motioned for them to go on without him.

Sarah made her way between her cousin and Grandpa, and reached the boutique.

Out front was parked an old, light-pink Cadillac, complete with tail fins.

"Grandma's here," Sarah said, smiling.

Emma and Sarah bounded up to Larry's apartment, taking the steps two at a time.

They rushed in, and in the kitchen, saw their grandma. Always a fashionable woman, she wore half-inch heels that made her look taller than she already was. Her slender, tanned arms were a stark contrast against her white top and bright red lipstick. Her sunglasses sat atop her head and a big grin was splashed across her face.

"Grandma!" Sarah exclaimed, rushing toward the woman she hadn't seen in such a long time.

"Sarah! Emma!"

Both of her granddaughters hugged her simultaneously, and Grandma chuckled. "Happy to see me, are you? What, did Larry put you through the wringer down in the shop?"

"Of course," Emma said.

Sarah laughed.

When Larry came in, Grandma and her granddaughters had concluded their embrace, and the woman sauntered over and gave him a hug.

"Lawrence," Grandma said, "thanks for holding down the fort—I see there's no signs of a kitchen fire this time."

"That was only once, Ruth," Larry said. He turned toward Emma and Sarah. "I swear, I'll never hear the end of it."

Grandma laughed. "You almost burned the whole building down making quiche."

"Exaggeration, much?"

Emma walked over and took her seat on the couch. "Was that the Quiche Quandary you told us about, Grandma?"

Sarah and Emma both laughed.

"Sure was," Grandma said. "So, did you girls enjoy the brownies I left you?"

Sarah and Emma glanced at one another, confused.

Grandma looked at Larry. "Lawrence, you told them about the brownies, didn't you?"

Larry stumbled over his words. "I...uh, what are you—"

Grandma waved her hand dismissively. "The ones I put in the freezer, remember?" She walked over to the refrigerator and opened the freezer section. "Oh, they're all gone. So, you did serve them..."

Larry's face was glowing red. "Yeah, I did."

He looked over at his granddaughters and shrugged.

"Now it all makes sense," Emma said. "The mystery of how Grandpa made brownies as good as Grandma has been officially put to bed."

"Case closed," Sarah chimed in.

The door to the apartment opened, and Adam rushed in. He said hello to Grandma, his face still neutral. Previously, he had been ecstatic to see the crazy, globetrotting grandma again, but now he was oddly reserved...

What was on Adam's mind?

Before Sarah could ask, Grandma spoke up: "What's wrong with you, Adam? Cat got your tongue?"

"I can't stay long," Adam said. "I just wanted to say hello to you, Mrs. Shores."

"What's going on?" Sarah said, stepping toward Adam. She could see that something was indeed wrong.

"They found a body," Adam blurted out.

Grandma's eyes grew wide, matching everyone else's expression.

"Another body?" Sarah asked.

Adam nodded. "At the Beachside Bed and Breakfast."

Larry said, "Looks like you and Sarah have more baddies to put away."

"Seems that way," Adam said. "But I don't want to spoil the party. I'll see you later, everyone. And Sarah, I'll be in touch."

Adam let himself out, and Sarah stood shocked. Another killer was on the loose in Cascade Cove. She knew what she had to do.

# # #

Thank you for reading! Want to help out?

Reviews are a big help for independent authors like me, so if you liked my book, **please consider leaving a review today**.

Thank you!

-Mel McCoy

Enjoy this Sneak Peek of Book 2!

CHAPTER 1

SARAH SHORES HEARD the waves crashing off to her left as she walked south along the boardwalk. Out for a walk with Winston and Rugby, she noticed that the beachside shops were open and bursting at the seams with tourists. The season was in full swing, and Sarah was excited to spend the rest of the summer in Cascade Cove, Florida.

"Easy, Rugby," she said, feeling the yellow lab pull slightly. To their right, coming toward them, a pair of Yorkshire terriers led an elderly couple along in the opposite direction.

The Yorkies yapped at Rugby, who pulled the lead more to say hello.

Sarah said hello to the couple, who seemed eager for their dogs to socialize. Winston, the corgi Sarah had rescued, pulled as well, joining Rugby in greeting the two miniature dogs.

Rugby's tail was going in overdrive as he sniffed at his new friends. His shadow eclipsed the two dogs, whose combined weight was only a fraction of the yellow lab's eighty pounds. Even Winston, who was nearly thirty pounds, outweighed their combined weight two-to-one.

"What're their names?" Sarah asked.

The woman smiled. "Penny and Jenny."

"You can tell who named them," the man said with a smirk.

Sarah laughed. "This is Rugby and Winston."

"We used to have a lab before we got these two runts," the old man said, bending down to pet Rugby and Winston.

"Oh, Carl," the woman said, swatting at him.

"Dolores likes small dogs."

Sarah peered down at the two Yorkies. "They are adorable."

"Thank you," Dolores said.

Sarah chatted with the couple for a few minutes while the dogs played, and then they said their goodbyes.

"Enjoy the rest of your day," Carl said, and he and his wife waved to Sarah and her dogs as they walked away.

"You too."

Sarah took a deep breath. The wind was warm, and the air was filled with the smell of saltwater, mixed with soft pretzels, cotton candy, and baked goods.

Up ahead, she spotted the Ferris wheel at the small amusement park, which was located at the southern end of the boardwalk. She smiled at the sight—it would be active later that evening, but now it stood motionless, teasing any passersby who might've been itching for a ride. The view from the top was breathtaking, she remembered, and she couldn't wait to ride the Ferris wheel again soon.

Though she'd been in Cascade Cove for two weeks—visiting her Grandpa and Grandma, along with her cousin, Emma—Sarah hadn't had a chance to ride the Ferris wheel.

Too many other things had gotten in the way...

Her mind drifted to the mysterious death of John Jacobs, a local landowner.

Sarah shook her head, ridding those thoughts from her mind. With that debacle behind the Cove, everything was back to normal, or so she hoped. Though Adam Dunkin told her a body had been found at The Beachside B&B, she didn't yet know the details.

Looking around, it didn't seem as if the town's occupants or tourists had caught wind of it.

The gossip mill wasn't churning, and Sarah was grateful.

"It'll get figured out," she muttered, guiding her dogs along. "Nothing can stop this busy season."

She walked her dogs down to the end of the board-walk, the Ferris wheel now towering over her.

She turned around and made her way back toward her grandpa's boutique. Once there, she went into Larry's Pawfect Boutique through the boardwalk-side entrance. Inside, she heard familiar voices.

"...and then the man did a belly-flop into the pool," Grandma was saying.

"Oh yeah?" came Adam's voice.

"We had to fish that sucker out of the pool—the belly-flop must've been by mistake, I suppose."

"*You* had to fish him out?"

"Well, not me...that's not what I do on those cruise ships. But one of the other staff members had to. The fellow was drunk as a sailor, if you can believe it."

Sarah let the dogs off their leashes, and they lunged toward Grandma and Adam.

"Oh look, Adam," Grandma said, "Sarah's back already."

Sarah strode up to her Grandma, giving her a big hug. "Hopefully they'll be conked out the rest of the morning."

Grandma chuckled. "If not, they'll drive your grandpa mad."

Ending their embrace, Sarah looked over to the

counter and saw Emma sitting on a stool, typing furiously on her laptop.

"Hey, Em," Sarah said.

Emma said something that resembled, "Hey," but didn't look up from her computer, nor did her typing speed slow in the least.

Sarah turned to Adam. "Aren't you on duty now?"

"He is," Grandma said, before Adam could get a word in, "but he's taking time out of his busy day to visit me, since he's such a sweetheart."

Adam's cheeks flushed slightly, and Sarah could tell that he was genuinely glad to hear that Grandma Shores still held him in high regard.

"Oh, Mrs. Shores," Adam said, waving dismissively.

Grandma wrapped her arms around him and squeezed hard, the same way she used to back when he was the boy who used to hang around Sarah and Emma all summer. When he would help them cause trouble around the Cove. Now, as a police officer in Cascade Cove, he was the one setting the troublemakers straight.

"So, Adam," Grandma said, smoothing out her white blouse. "Tell us, what's going on with that body they found at The Beachside B&B?"

Sarah's eyes went wide and she could see Emma perk up from her computer. Her cousin could never pass up information about a body found or a mystery. But Sarah couldn't believe how blunt her grandmother was being. She could now see where her cousin got it from. "Grandma!"

Grandma looked at Sarah. "What?"

"It's okay," Adam said. He turned to Grandma. "I can tell you this much: We found a body and it happened the other night at Cecil's bed and breakfast."

"That's it?" Grandma waved her hand at Adam.

Adam pulled out his notepad from his pocket and flipped it open to a random page, making a show of it.

"The victim is male," he said, then flipped the notebook closed again and put it back in his pocket.

Grandma put her hands on her hips, waiting. "And?"

Adam chuckled. "Mrs. Shores, you know I can't tell you much more than that."

"Bah." Grandma waved her hand at Adam again. "You're no fun."

Emma let out a huff and slid from her stool. "You guys are boring me. I'm going to go upstairs to grab a chocolate chip cookie." She looked at Adam. "I made them last night. You want one?"

It was known around Cascade Cove that Emma didn't share the same talent in the kitchen as her grandma or grandpa. Sarah could see the look of muted trepidation on Adam's face, which matched Grandma's deer-in-the-headlights gaze.

"Uh, no thanks," Adam said. "I've got to get going soon. But thanks."

"Anyone else?"

Sarah and Grandma looked at each other, hoping the other would take one for the team, but they both said "no" in unison.

Grandma added, "Don't want to spoil my dinner, dear."

Nice save, Sarah thought to herself.

"Suit yourself," Emma said, sauntering to the door that led to the upstairs apartment.

Once Emma was surely out of earshot, Sarah asked Grandma, "No cookies for you?"

Grandma shook her head. "That girl needs to learn how to read a recipe."

Sarah and Adam laughed.

Grandma, not paying any mind to them, stepped over to the counter where Emma had sat and ran a finger along the top. She furrowed her brow and wiped her fingers together quickly, to get any dust off. "You know, Cecil and Larry go way back," she said to nobody in particular.

"Oh yeah?" Adam asked.

"Yeah, they used to go bowling together every Friday night. They had a bowling team. What was their name... oh yeah, the Rock Lobsters."

Adam chuckled.

"What?"

"Nothing. So, do they still have the team?"

"No."

"Why not?"

"No reason. Just that Cecil started running a bed and breakfast, and with Larry having the pet boutique…You know how it goes. Just didn't leave much time for them."

"That's too bad," Sarah said.

Grandma nodded. "That's just how life is. People drift in and out of our lives."

"Well," Adam said, "I hate to cut this short, but I really do have to get back to the station."

"See you, sweetheart," Grandma said, giving Adam one final hug before he hurried out the front of the store, back to where his police cruiser was likely parked on the main strip.

Grandma grabbed a rag from under the counter and ran it along the top of the counter.

Sarah said, "I didn't know Grandpa was on a bowling team."

"Who's in charge of dusting this place?"

"I mean, it makes sense…I can see him right at home at a bowling alley, with his Hawaiian shirt and all."

Grandma looked at the rag and grimaced. "Well, it was a while ago. I think you were in college at the time."

Before Sarah could reply, she heard pounding footsteps above them, and yelling. Something was going on upstairs.

Sarah whipped her head toward the front of the store, in time to see Emma rushing into the boutique, frantic.

"What's wrong?" Sarah asked.

"There's a fire in the kitchen!"

Sarah's eyes went wide, and she glanced at her grandma, who also wore a look of disbelief.

"A fire?"

# # #

To be continued in Book Two

ABOUT THE AUTHOR

Mel McCoy has had a lifelong love of mysteries of all kinds. Reading everything from Nancy Drew to the Miss Marple series and obsessed with shows like *Murder, She Wrote*, her love of the genre has never wavered.

Now she is hoping to spread her love of mysteries through her new Whodunit Pet Cozy Mystery Series. Centered around a cozy beachside town, the series features a cast of interesting characters and their pets, along with antiques, crafts such as knitting, and plenty of culinary delights.

For more info on Mel McCoy's cozy mystery series, please visit: www.melmccoybooks.com

CPSIA information can be obtained
at www.ICGtesting.com
Printed in the USA
BVHW041106270519
549332BV00024B/2153/P

9 781096 695868